THE JUDGE IS REVERSED

The Judge Is Reversed

A Mr. and Mrs. North Mystery

BY

FRANCES AND RICHARD
LOCKRIDGE

J. B. LIPPINCOTT COMPANY
Philadelphia　　　　　　　New York

00162 709 3

THE JUDGE IS REVERSED

I

THERE WAS, Pamela North said, no use waiting to be adopted. "Because," she said, "of the elevator. It's asking too much."

She said this across the breakfast table, on a bright morning in early September. Jerry said, "Um-m-m" and, "Somebody ought to teach him a second service" and then, "What, Pam?" When he said the last he looked up from the folded newspaper stretched beside his plate.

Pam did not repeat, but only waited for seepage, which she assumed to be inevitable. Momentarily, her words lay on a mind's surface, like drops of water on dry soil. They would penetrate.

"The elevator does complicate it," Jerry North said. "You're ready, then?"

"Yes," she said. "It's empty the way it is. Of course, there'll never be another—"

He smiled at her; smiled tenderly.

"All right," Pam said. "Take it as unsaid. All the same, it's true."

"Of course," Jerry said. "Nor was there another Pete. Another Ruffy. Each one is different. It's a matter of luck. You cross your fingers and take a chance."

He waited for her to nod her head. She didn't "puddle up," any more. So it was time for the next cat.

"You're right about not being adopted," he said. "Sitting on a doorstep. Yes. Any cat may be expected to do that. But not coming up in the elevator."

Pete, who was the first cat, had sat, in the rain, on a stoop in the Village, waited to be rescued, spoken of discomfort, and been a kitten then. That had been long ago, when the Norths had lived in a walk-up. Pete had been black and white.

"Anyway," Jerry said, "Siamese don't adopt much. Unless?"

"Oh," Pam said, "I think so. If we can find some who aren't too pointed."

She meant of face. Jerry knew she meant of face. When things have been said often enough, they go without further saying. Jerry said, "So?"

"Sampling," Pam said. "You want to sample with me?"

He raised eyebrows.

"The fifty-third annual championship show of the Colony Cat Club," Pam said. "All breeds. There's a story about it in the *Times*. At the Burnside. The last day."

"No," Jerry said. "Author trouble."

She said, "Bad?"

He shrugged.

"Lunch," he said. "Soothing of ruffled feathers. They're feathery beasts."

"Whose second service?" Pam asked him, and this time he all but missed—said "Wh—" and then, "Oh."

"Doug Mears's," he said. "Double-faulted eleven times in one set. Won it but—Al Laney's very cross about it. In the *Herald Trib*."

"Mr. Laney's often cross," Pam said. "Are we going out tomorrow? Or will there be authors in the way?"

"On Saturday?" Jerry said, in some astonishment. Pam said, a little absently, that she supposed authors had Saturdays, like anybody else. "Not," Jerry told her, and now was grim, "on my time."

He looked at his watch, then, and said, "Good God," in a tone of surprise. Always, Pam North thought, he felt the same surprise, expressed it so. And always at about the same time of morning. It is pleasant, Pam thought, to be sure of things. It provides continuity.

Jerry went, leaning slightly to starboard under the weight of brief case full of manuscript. It was amazing, when one stopped to think of it, how long books were getting. Pam stopped only briefly to think of it. She poured herself more coffee, and read Mr. Al Laney, in the New York *Herald Tribune*, on the fourth-round matches in the national championships at Forest Hills. Mr. Laney was, indeed, very cross. He was cross not so much at Doug Mears, who had offended, as at his mentors, who let him continue to hit his second service as hard, and as flat, as his first. No good would come of that, Mr. Laney felt. If young players, and especially young players as promising as Doug Mears, were not better advised by their elders, the Davis Cup would remain in Australia for the foreseeable future. Mr. Laney evidently thought this would be very bad for it.

Pam turned from Mr. Laney to Mr. Walter Lippmann, who also was having a dark day. It was time, Pam decided, to glance at Mr. David Lawrence, whose column she habitually takes in small, therapeutic doses. A paragraph or two of Lawrence, taken with coffee, raises the blood pressure and arouses the mind, eliminating any possible trace of morning lethargy. Overdosage must, of course, be avoided, as of any counter-irritant.

Pam abandoned Mr. Lawrence when she felt the first glow of rage, said "Yah!" in his general direction, and went to clothe herself. She left a note for Martha—they would need more coffee and all the lemons in the refrigerator were naked, so they would need more lemons—and went down the elevator (which cats could not be expected to use) into the bright crispness of the September day. She wrapped the brightness around her, knowing it transient, and walked half a dozen blocks before she took a cab to the Hotel Burnside, which had a ballroom full of cats.

Pam paid at the desk, bought a catalogue, and walked among cages to look at cats. She was, in turn, looked at—looked at, distantly, through yellow eyes and green eyes, blue eyes and amber. Cats in cages crouched on cushions, nibbled from food dishes, scratched be-

[9]

hind ears. But mostly, Pam felt, they looked at her—at her and the other people who walked between the rows of cages. Of course, she thought. The cats are attending a people show. How nice for them. Her mind checked. Perhaps, on the other hand, it wasn't nice for them at all. A dull breed, the cats might think; a dull gray breed in monochrome.

The cats came in a variety of design, and this fact, which should not have surprised Pam North, was so dramatized by feline multitude that it did somewhat startle her. Black and white cats are to be anticipated; yellow cats are numerous enough and almost all cats run a little to tabby stripings. But these cats nevertheless dazzled. Some of the cats called "blue" were, indeed, almost blue in glossy fur; silver cats glimmered in the shadow of their cages. And the black cats wore jewels for eyes.

The trouble with the long-hairs, Pam found herself thinking, is that they are a little showy. Beautiful but—unrestrained. This one, she thought—pausing to look into a cage at a red tabby—really carries things too far. "Pretty kitty," Pam said, absently, to the red tabby, who reclined on what appeared to be velvet. Pretty kitty turned away her head. Or his head. Number 181, pretty kitty was, and Pam looked the number up in the catalogue. She read, "Morland's Enchanted Lady of Purrland, Dbl.Ch. Kute Kit Monarch of Purrland ex Lady Four Paws Beautiful of Purrland. Br-own Miss Rebecca Wuerth."

"Goodness," Pam North said, aloud but not especially to Enchanted Lady of Purrland. It had to be said to someone. "Poor Kitty," Pam said, this time to the red tabby. What cats must think of people who named them so!

"If you please," a thin voice said and Pam turned. The voice came from under a hat made of pink flowers. It came from between colorless lips in a sallow face. The woman who spoke wore a long black dress with—*with fringe*. Pam felt that she had wasted her "Goodness." This, if ever, was the time for it. "*If* you please," the woman said again and, assuming that to be desired, Pam moved away from Enchanted Lady's cage. The woman in black and pink—and fringe! —opened Enchanted Lady's cage and took the cat out of it. The woman found a stool and, from somewhere in the black dress, a brush and a comb. Without speaking to the cat, she began to brush her. The cat was equally without comment.

There couldn't be much fun in it for anybody, Pam North thought, and smiled at the sallow woman in the pink—my God, why pink?—hat and was looked through. Pam went on, seeking Siamese. Siamese would, without doubt, have something to say.

She found them presently—a long row of Siamese. She spoke to the nearest, and was instantly spoken to. Thata-cat, Pam thought, and looked closer. A seal point, beautifully marked, sinuous even in repose, with a tail like a long brown whip—and, with a face that came to a point. "You poor thing," Pam said, and sighed.

You spoke to cats and people also answered.

"Why?" a woman asked Pam North. "Why poor thing? A double grand champion. Why a poor thing?"

This woman was much younger and wore no hat at all; she wore a tweed suit of soft brown; she had pale hair and a pink face. And she was too large, too sturdy a woman for a tweed suit. Which was her business, not Pam's.

"Oh," Pam said. "A prejudice. I know they're bred for pointed faces nowadays. I just wish they weren't." She looked down the Siamese row. "And they all are," she said. "It makes it very difficult."

The woman in the tweed suit repeated the last word. She had a robust voice.

"I'm sampling," Pam said. "Mine—ours—" She paused momentarily. "Died," she said. It still wasn't easy to say. "She had a round face," Pam said. "A baby face." She looked again at the lithe double

[11]

grand champion. "She looked like a cat," Pam said. "I think they should."

"They're supposed to have wedge-shaped faces," the woman in tweed said, and was somewhat impatient.

"A wedge," Pam North said, with conviction, "isn't a cone."

It was a last word. Pam was not sure it was precisely the word she wanted, but there is no use arguing with people who—presumably—show cats. "Anyway," Pam said, as one more word, and started to move down the row of cages.

"You're looking for a cat," the tweed woman said. "Perhaps I can help you. Sometimes they—revert. Even in the best lines— I'm Madeline Somers."

It seemed to Pam that the expected answer to that probably was "Not *really?*" She could not manage it. She said, "I'm Pamela North," with no thought that Madeline Somers would care particularly. It was merely a matter of fair exchange.

"Not *really!*" Madeline Somers said, heartily. Pam looked at her with widened eyes.

"*The* Mrs. North," Madeline Somers said, and this time with triumph. Pam blinked her eyes, involuntarily. "The—" Madeline Somers said and stopped abruptly. "The—" Miss Somers repeated, but with obviously less confidence. "Wait," Miss Somers said, and Pam waited. "Criminologist!" Miss Somers said, triumph regained. And to this Pam, after a little shuffling of her mind, could only say, "Oh." She shuffled further. "Not really," she said.

"You and your husband," Miss Somers said. "Don't tell me. He's—wait. He's a publisher, but you and he are private—"

"No," Pam said. "I suppose you mean detective. Or maybe eyes. We're not at all. It's only that—" It was her turn to pause. As years had passed, it had grown more difficult. The fault of the newspapers, Pam thought. "All it is," she said, "we know a detective. It—the rest just seems to happen." It wasn't adequate. "Somehow," Pam North added, not feeling she made it any clearer. "Once," she said, "we found a body in a bathtub. That's all there was to it, really."

Madeline Somers looked down at Pam North. After a moment, she said, "Well." Pam saw her point, but did not feel that there was anything to be done about it.

"You are in the market for a cat?" Madeline Somers said, and became brisk again. "A Siamese?"

"If not too pointed," Pam said. "I came here just—well, to see if there was anything new in cats. A—a new fall line, I suppose."

Madeline Somers blinked slightly.

"I sell cats," she said. "Breeders' Nook."

"Breeders'—?"

"Here," Madeline Somers said, and opened her show program and thrust it toward Pam, a finger marking. The finger marked an advertisement.

The Breeders' Nook
Registered Persians, Siamese, Abyssinians
Burmese—all breeds. Cheetahs Sometimes
Available. Ocelots may be ordered.
Madeline Somers. —— Madison Avenue.

"Goodness," Pam said. "Not cheetahs?"

"Well," Madeline Somers said, "I don't argue there's much demand. Big for apartments. And ocelots get chest colds, of course. But—you don't want an ocelot, probably."

"A pet shop," Pam said. She could not keep doubt out of her voice. The Norths are by no means of what cat people call The Fancy. But still—pet shops?

"Not the way you mean," Madeline Somers said. "Oh, I know what you mean. These are all registered cats, from good breeders. More like a—say a cat exchange. A clearing house." Pam looked up

[13]

at her. "Oh," the tweeded woman said, "I don't contend they're all show types. But I take it you don't want a cat to show."

"No," Pam said. "To talk to. To—talk with."

"A Siamese," Madeline Somers said, with understanding. "I've got—"

"Outrageous," a thin, high voice—a piercing voice—said from somewhere. "Incompetence. Or worse."

They turned to look toward the voice's source. It was the kind of voice which, in itself, somehow creates a situation. Only an emergency could justify such a voice. The lithe seal point at whom Pam had first looked rose from his folded blanket. He growled deep in his throat.

They were near an open section, in which a good many people—mostly women—were already gathered. The voice came from there, pierced out from there. A woman in a long black dress—a dress with fringe—stood on one side of a table and looked up at a tall man. The tall man was slim, erect; he had a tanned face and regular features; he had gray hair. Over a dark suit, he wore, somewhat unexpectedly, a butcher's apron. It was immaculate; it was still inappropriate. White tie and tails—the man suggested that.

There were half a dozen portable cages on the table in front of the little woman—the sallow, wiry little woman in the fringed dress, the equally improbable pink hat. Medallioned ribbons lay on two of the cages.

"Don't think I don't know," the woman in the black dress said, and her voice cut. "Don't think you can pull the wool over my eyes. Call yourself a judge—"

"Poor Becky Wuerth," Madeline Somers said. "Somebody ought to do something. The poor thing. And poor John Blanchard, too."

Pam raised eyebrows.

"The all-breeds judge," Miss Somers said. "Here." She opened her catalogue again, again a finger marked. "Judge: Mr. John Blanchard."

"They were lucky to get him," Miss Somers said. "And now poor Becky Wuerth."

"I take it," Pam said, "that her cat didn't win."

"Apparently," Miss Somers said. "The trouble is, hers usually don't. And if it's Enchanted Lady again—well, Lady is just a pretty red. Why Becky thinks—" She paused. She smiled faintly. "Actually," she said, "most of them—I suppose I ought to be honest and say us—suspect dirty work at the crossroads when we don't win the blues. Partly pride—partly just admiration of their own cats. Our own cats. But for the breeders—well, money enters in. Stud fees. The prices kittens will bring. So—judges are incompetent. At best, as poor Becky shouted. At worst—you ought to hear them, Mrs. North."

"If you think you're going—" Rebecca Wuerth, indignant owner of Enchanted Lady of Purrland, daughter of Dbl.Ch. Kute Kit Monarch of Purrland and Lady Four Paws Beautiful, began, her voice a knife in the air. But then a comfortable woman in a blue dress came up behind her and made soothing sounds in a soft voice. "All the same," Rebecca Wuerth said. "If he thinks he's heard the last—"

She did not finish. She went away; Pam felt that she was more or less led away. The tall, spare man in the butcher's apron had said nothing; had not seemed to hear. Now he motioned, and two men carried caged cats from the judging table.

"Class forty-four," a public-address system said. "Blue male novice."

The two men who had carried caged cats away returned with new caged cats—four caged cats.

The tall man took a cat from a cage. The cat dangled. Then the cat wrapped himself around the judge's hands. The tall man shook slightly, and put the cat on the table. The cat was very handsome,

[15]

long-haired, amber eyes. He permitted the tall man to run hands over him, hold his tail extended; lift him and gaze into his eyes. The judge put the cat back in his cage and lifted another blue from the next cage. The group which had watched the earlier judging drifted away; a new group drifted in.

The tall man was very deft with cats. Still, Pam thought, judging cats must be rather a risky business—cats are edged tools.

"Don't they ever bite him?" Pam asked. "Or scratch, for that matter?"

"Now and then, I suppose," Madeline Somers said. "But he's very good with them. The chief risk is cat hair on clothes. Hence the apron."

"All the same," Pam said, "it seems like an odd—occupation. For a man, especially."

"Occupation?" Miss Somers repeated, as if the word surprised her. It seemed also to amuse her. She chuckled. "He would love that," she said. "You mean you've never heard of John Blanchard?"

Pam North had never heard of John Blanchard. Not then.

II

Pam didn't, she told Jerry, know that the sampling had helped much. "Like," she said, "a smorgasbord. Confusing. And not taking something because there may be something even better on down."

"And," Jerry said, "ending up with cold turkey. I know."

"More likely with everything," Pam said. "Burmese are nice. And the long-hairs—"

"No," Jerry said. "Brushing, chiefly. If not, hair balls in the cat and knots on him. Were all the Siamese pointed?"

They had been. On the other hand, there was the chance of Madeline Somers's shop. Now and then, apparently, it contained an unpointed Siamese.

"Although probably," Pam said, "with black stripes."

They had, at that moment, entered the Queens-Midtown tunnel. The tunnel roared around them.

"Stripes?" Jerry enquired, loudly.

"Belly stripes," Pam said. "Although I don't know that we care, do we? Do you know a Mr. John Blanchard? It seems everybody ought to. He judges cats."

"When we get out of this," Jerry said. Jerry yelled.

They got out of it. In time, they got to Queens Boulevard.

"There was a Blanchard wrote a book about cats," Jerry said. "That's about all I know. Very good book, they say. Compared it to Van Vechten, some did."

"Nonsense," Pam said firmly. "How ridiculous. A tall, thin man, in his late fifties? Gray hair? I suppose you'd have to call him distinguished-looking?"

"All I know about him," Jerry said, "is that he wrote a book about cats. Nothing about his dimensions. If it's the same man. And, why, Pam?"

Pam didn't know. It had seemed an odd thing for a man to be doing. Naturally, she had wondered, mildly, about the man. It was unimportant. "We turn left at the next corner," she said.

A canvas sign which crossed the boulevard told them they turned left at the next corner. They turned left; they found a parking area; they climbed concrete steps into the concrete oval of the stadium, came out into bright sunlight; were shown places on a ribbed bench. Far below, on tattered turf, young men in white ran and leaped. "Game, Mr. Mears," a loudspeaker told them. "He leads, five games to four, first set."

The young men in white met, and mopped, behind the umpire's chair. They went back on court, the courts reversed. Now the player nearest the Norths was a rangy man, his close-cropped blond hair shining in the sun.

"Mears," Jerry said. "The one Laney's cross with."

Mears raised a hand which held two tennis balls.

"New balls," Jerry said. "And, he's obviously got a break through. And—"

"Shhh," Pam said.

Mears's long body seemed to lash like a whip, with a whip's snap at the end. The ball fled.

"Wow!" Pam North said, in appreciation. The dark-haired man on the far side of the net shook his head, waggled his racket in doleful appreciation. "Fifteen—love," the umpire said, through the public-address system.

Doug Mears served again. This time the ball came back, drifting high. Mears smashed. "Thirty—love," the public-address system said.

The crowd was very silent. Somewhere, off to the side, a typewriter clicked. The dark-haired man went back to position, waited

[18]

to receive. He moved lithely as he waited, shifting weight, like a cat tensing for a spring.

Mears served again. The ball was a white streak into court, breaking wide. The dark-haired man lunged and missed.

"Foot fault," a voice said, and was loud in the silence. "Foot fault," the loudspeaker repeated.

Everybody looked at the base-line judge. Mears looked at him in apparent astonishment, disbelief. He looked at him for seconds which seemed minutes. The linesman did not seem to look at him.

Mears shook his head, in resignation, yet with anger.

"Third one this set," a man next Pam said to her, in a hushed voice. "Upsets the kid."

Mears served again. The ball, this time, hit the net cord, bounced high. "Let" the net judge called. "Out," a linesman called, and made a sweeping gesture of the left hand. "Double fault," the umpire's amplified voice told a crowd of some eight thousand. "Thirty—fifteen."

Mears served again, but the whip of his body seemed less certain. He went in behind service. The ball from the dark-haired man's racket streaked past him, deep down the line. The silence was palpable. It was unbroken. Mears turned and looked at the base linesman—the same linesman. The linesman did not look at him.

"Thirty—all," the umpire said, and Jerry said, "Looked out from here."

"Looked out to Mears, too," said the man on the other side of Pam, across her. "But John knows his job."

Pam had looked at the linesman quickly, without really looking. She looked again.

He wore slacks and a dark jacket. He was sitting, now on the hardness of a folding wooden chair. He was lean and elegant still; his hair was thick and gray.

"Jerry!" Pam North said, and Jerry, this time, said "Shhh!"

Mears's swinging racket pinged on the ball, and the ball flew.

There was a faint sigh from the crowd, even before the linesman called. "Fault," the loudspeaker said, imperturbable, and Mears served again. He seemed to serve harder than before. The ball streaked down the center of the court, landed on, or near, the center line. "Fault," the center linesman of the far court said, and the loudspeaker said, "Double fault, thirty—forty."

Mears went back to position, shaking his blond head from side to side. He looked, suddenly, tired. He served, and the ball tore into the far court. "Let," the net judge said. "First service," the loudspeaker said. Mears served again, and this time the ball, angled toward the side line, went far beyond it. "Fault." Mears, walking back, moved slowly. The whip of his body coiled again, snapped again.

"Foot fault," the man in slacks and dark jacket, the man with thick gray hair, said, clearly in the silence. There was, this time, a pause. It was as if the loudspeaker hesitated. "Double fault," the loudspeaker said. "Game, Mr. Wilson. The games are five all, first set."

And Doug Mears banged his racket on the ground—banged it down twice on the battered turf. He started toward the linesman, and seemed to be talking, although his words were not audible. A kind of moan from the audience drowned the words.

Mears took two long strides, and the linesman did not look at him. Mears stopped, then, and his shoulders sagged. He went back to receive. He went very slowly, as if each step were an effort.

"Bad break for the kid," the man next Pam said. "Sometimes a thing like that'll—" He did not finish. The dark-haired man had served. The ball bounced crookedly. Mears, obviously off balance, swung awkwardly. The ball hit the net. "Some days it's not worth while getting up," the man next Pam said. "What a bounce!"

Crossing to receive in the backhand court, the blond young man looked fixedly at the linesman in dark jacket, dark slacks. The man did not appear to look at him.

Mears made the next point on a dipping return of service. But on the point which followed a similar return was lobbed over his head and, from thirty—fifteen, Mears volleyed once into the net and once far beyond the base line.

"Game, Mr. Wilson. He leads, six games to five, first set."

As the players changed courts, Doug Mears stopped at the umpire's high chair, spoke up to the umpire; spoke with apparent vehemence, once gestured toward the base linesman. The umpire listened. The umpire shook his head.

Mears won the first point of the twelfth game on a service ace. But he double-faulted the second, dumped a volley—a volley that looked, from the stands, easy—into the net and then, once more, double-faulted. At fifteen—forty, Wilson—Ted Wilson, it turned out to be—put up a short lob off a strong service and Mears smashed.

He smashed with a kind of fury, angling the ball. It landed inches beyond the side line, bounced hard and true—bounced spitefully toward the base linesman. The linesman moved, moved quickly. He caught the ball and for a moment held it in his hand, looking at it as if it were a strange object, an inimical object. Then he tossed it toward a ballboy and stood up, and looked the length of the court at Doug Mears. He looked for some seconds, and sat down again.

"Game and first set, Mr. Wilson," the loudspeaker said, in a silence which was curiously sodden. Then, and only then, the audience applauded, but not as if its heart was in applause.

"If I can say something now without shush," Pam said. "Judge not that ye be not judged. In other words, that's Mr. Blanchard. First cats and then feet. First a woman in fringe, and then poor Mr. Mears."

"Thirty—love," the loudspeaker said.

"Poor Mr. Mears," Pam said again, watching Ted Wilson's third service go for an ace—for an ace at which Mears lunged with no apparent enthusiasm.

"I've heard about the cats," the man on Pam's right said. He had, apparently, joined them. At tennis matches, spectators are comrades under the skin. "Always think of old Johnny as a tennis man, myself. Used to be—"

"Oh," Jerry said. "*That* Blanchard."

Pam looked from one to the other.

"Thirty years ago," Jerry said, "he was one of the good ones."

"Almost," the other man said.

"All right, almost. Quarter finals at Wimbledon, wasn't it?"

"Semis," the other man said. "But he was senior champion three years straight not so long ago. Now he's an umpire, mostly. Filling in on lines today, but he's usually in the chair. Calls them as he sees them, Johnny does. The kid let it get him. Too bad, because he figured to take—"

"Game, Mr. Wilson. He leads, one game to love, second set."

"—which would have put him in line for a pro bid," the informant on Pam's right said. "Now—but it could be he'll snap out of it."

Mears did not. He was broken through in the second game, and Wilson coasted to six-three. Each time he served from the base line Blanchard watched, as linesman and foot-fault judge; Doug Mears glared at the older man. And from that side, he served badly, seemed uncertain—looked after each service again at Blanchard, and seemed to wait.

"He's let it get him," the authority on Pam's right said. "He's sure enough let it get him."

Mears played better in the third set, but not enough better. It went to Wilson at seven-five. The match went with it.

"Mr. Wilson is good," Pam said, as they went down the concrete steps.

"Not that good," Jerry told her. "As our friend said, Mears let it get him."

"What, exactly, is a foot fault?"

"God only knows," Jerry said.

"And Mr. Blanchard," Pam said. "He knows." They went into the garden bar and found a table. And waited. And continued to wait. When she came, the waitress was sorry, and would bring gins and tonics.

They waited, without impatience. At Forest Hills in tournament time only the players hurry. They hurry enough for everybody. It was pleasant in the garden bar, at an umbrella-shaded table among other tables scattered on grass—tables now filling during the intermission between stadium matches. Half a dozen men sat at a long table, and gestured tennis as they drank; along a path between the tables and the field courts, brisk young people in white walked back and forth and one could guess whether they were participants in the nationals or merely passive members of the West Side Tennis Club. It was Pam's theory, advanced while they waited, that people carrying only two tennis rackets were probably not in the tournament. At least not at this stage.

"It takes," she said, "three rackets and a serious expression. Here he is again."

Jerry looked where she looked.

"I begin to feel I'm being followed," Pam said.

John Blanchard, authority on cats and, it now appeared, tennis, was not alone. With him was a slender and sprightly girl in white shorts and blouse and sweater—a very pretty girl, who seemed to sparkle as she walked beside the much taller, much older man; a girl with deep red hair. They turned from the path and passed quite close to the Norths on their way to a table. "—ought to apologize," the girl said, smiling up to the man. Blanchard shook his head at her and shrugged slightly, square shoulders moving under dark

[23]

jacket. As they passed the long table of men who talked tennis with their hands, one of them—who had, as far as one could guess, been demonstrating the proper forehand—broke it off to salute Blanchard and to say "Hiya, Johnny?" At that there was a low chorus of "hiyas" and one "You can lose your head thataway, Johnny," at which there was general laughter.

Blanchard waved and did not answer, but his regular features moved into a regular smile. He touched the girl's brown arm, guiding her to a table under an umbrella.

The waitress came to the Norths' table, and said she was sorry to have been so long, and deposited gins and tonics and said "Thank you" for a tip and went. From his table, Blanchard beckoned to her, and she went there. The Norths sipped, sitting in the sun. From beyond the fence—from the grandstand, probably—there was hand clapping. Somebody had done something which could be approved. The Norths sipped on.

And then a rangy young man in tennis shorts and sweater, carrying rackets, came down the path. He came without looking to either side, his expression set—his expression angry. When he was at a place where he could see all the tables in the garden bar he stopped, and looked at all of them. And then, his face more set than ever, he walked over grass, walked to the table at which Blanchard and the girl were sitting. When he got to it he stopped and glared down at Blanchard. After some seconds, he looked at the girl, and then back at Blanchard.

Everybody in the small enclosure stopped talking. Somebody put a glass down, and the sound of the glass on the metal table top was like a tiny explosion in the silence.

"Well," Doug Mears said, and spoke loudly, with a grating in his voice. "It worked out fine, didn't it, Blanchard? *Mr.* Blanchard."

There was a peculiar emphasis when he said "Mr." It was as if he derided the appellation as applied to the man he spoke to.

[24]

Blanchard merely looked up at him, as if he looked through him. He lifted his glass and drank from it, and put it down on the table.

"Doug!" the girl said. *"Doug!"*

The rangy man looked at her again, and looked away again.

Everybody watched. One of the men at the long table stood up, and started to move around the table toward Doug Mears and Blanchard and the girl.

"Got just what you went after, didn't you?" Mears said, and his voice was still loud, harsh. "Think you did, anyway. Got it sitting right here and—"

Blanchard stood up, then. He moved very quickly when he moved.

"I'd stop there, Mears," Blanchard said. His voice was not as loud as the younger man's—the much younger man's. But his voice bit in the silence. "I'd stop right there."

"You'd like me to," Mears said. "You're a prize son of a bitch, *Mr.* Blanchard. A lousy, creepy old—"

Blanchard came around the table then. And then the man who had started seconds before from the long table came up behind Doug Mears and put a hand hard on the blond man's shoulder and said, "I'd knock it off, son."

The pretty girl put her elbows on the table and her face in her hands, and the dark red hair streamed down around her face.

Doug Mears wheeled, his face working.

"I'll—" he began.

"You'll knock it off," the man who held him said. "You're off the beam, son. Way off. So far off that—"

He did not finish, but looked steadily at Doug Mears. And, after some moments, Mears shrugged and the man removed his hand from Mears's shoulder. He said, "Thata-boy."

"What you mean is," Mears said, but his voice was lower. "What you mean is—be a good boy, take it lying down or—or get suspended. Ruled off the—"

"Now son," the man said, and spoke like a father. "Why don't you just run along? Probably nobody'll remember hearing anything." He looked across at Blanchard, still standing, flush showing under the tan of his face. He looked and seemed to wait, and after some moments Blanchard nodded his head briefly, and sat down. The girl did not move, still hid her face in hands and soft, dark-red hair.

Doug Mears looked for a moment at the man who had intervened. Then he looked once more, his face dark, at Blanchard, who met his gaze; whose face showed no expression of any kind. Mears wrenched free of the restraining hand then, and walked across the grass to the path, looking at nobody, and then walked away along the path. Everybody watched him—everybody except John Blanchard and the girl with him. Blanchard was talking, his voice inaudible, to the girl, who, after a time began shaking her head slowly, without moving the hands which hid her face.

The loudspeaker in the stadium was even louder here, it seemed, than within the enclosure itself. It spoke now. "Linesmen ready?" it enquired, asking the rhetorical question—and, evidently, being greeted by the traditional silence. "Play," the loudspeaker roared.

Pam finished her drink and said, "Come on," and stood, and Jerry finished his and went with her across the grass to the path. "Although," Pam said, "almost anything will be an anticlimax, won't it? What's all this about its being only a game? And I want a hot dog."

They stopped under the stadium for hot dogs and carried them up the steep stairway. "Game, Mr. Farthing," the loudspeaker said. "He leads, one game to love, first set."

Again lithe young men raced on green, performing prodigious feats with rackets and with balls. The Norths munched and watched, and then, after wiping mustard from faces, merely watched. It was a better match than the other, and nobody seemed especially enraged, although there was the usual amount of hopeless headshaking over shots gone wrong and, from Dennis Farthing an occasional admiring and audible "Wow!" in appreciation of an opponent's ace. Mr. Farthing, being an Australian, won, but it took him five sets and only the last was easy.

John Blanchard did not officiate and, although Pam thought she saw him sitting under the marquee, she could not be sure. If the man was Blanchard, he was alone.

They stayed for several games of the mixed doubles match which followed, on Pam's theory that they might learn something. But when the members of one team found themselves simultaneously in a distant corner of the court, imperiling each other with swinging rackets, Pam said she thought they had learned enough. "After all," she said, "we could do that. And have."

"When we could run faster," Jerry agreed, but agreed also that it was time to go.

Driving home, Pam North kept remembering young Doug Mears.

"Grant he was disappointed," she said. "Grant he was mad. Still —to get as mad as all that? Of course, I suppose the girl is mixed up in it, somehow. They tend to get. Particularly when—did you think she was pretty, Jerry?"

"I didn't," Gerald North said, gravely, "notice especially."

"What a lie," Pam said. "And how nice of you to bother to tell it. Makes me feel so—nurtured. Unless you're slipping?"

Jerry said, "mmm?"

"I didn't say you were," Pam said. "Is Mears an especially temperamental player, do you know?"

"Never saw him play before," Jerry said, clipping words because of trucks. "Hadn't heard that. Did blow up."

"Did he really mean to hit Mr. Blanchard with that smash?"

"How'd I know?"

"It looked like it," Pam said. "And afterward, with his fists. Is it that important for them to win?"

[27]

"Some of them," Jerry said, "damn it all, stay in line." This was to a truck, which had not. "This Mears—supposed to beat Wilson easy. Good chance against Farthing, who'll gobble Wilson. Mears had won, probably got pro offer. Now nope. For God's sake make up your mind."

Pam sorted correctly, since she had had practice. She said, "Even a pro offer?"

"Depends," Jerry said. "Guarantee's gone as high as fifty thousand for the first year. Could be, Mears lost that in less than a couple of hours. Irritating, sort of."

"It would me," Pam said. "And blamed Mr. Blanchard. Who seems to get a good deal of blame. Speaking of cats—"

They spoke of cats, when Jerry was not speaking to other drivers, for some time. They decided to be resolute against pointed ones.

III

AL LANEY, writing in the *Herald Tribune*, hit the nail most precisely on the head, Jerry North said, and read applicable sections aloud to Pam, who was reading the *Times* and displayed forbearance and a modicum of attention.

"Doug Mears, one of the most promising of our younger players, lost a good deal yesterday," Jerry read from the works of Mr. Laney. "He lost a match he should have won easily, his temper and, probably, whatever chance he may have had of a bid to join the professional ranks this year. He revealed that he lacked the one essential of a really good player—the ability to concentrate on the point in play and to remain unruffled by adverse decisions."

That there had been cause for young Mr. Mears to become upset, Mr. Laney admitted. More foot faults had been called against him in a single set than against any player in Mr. Laney's memory, with the possible exception of one famous incident, which Mr. Laney did remember. On the other hand, the calls had been made by John Blanchard, an official of long experience—although more often seen in the umpire's chair than on a line—and unquestionable impartiality. Relaxed as the foot rule had become, it remained a rule, and not one which could be ignored. "It is the opinion of most observers," Mr. Laney wrote, "that Mears has for a long time ignored it flagrantly, and that he is not alone in this."

It was, admittedly, unfortunate that the calls came on crucial points, at moments when Mears had been close to running out the first set. But this did not justify the young man's open display of anger, culminating in what looked uncomfortably like a smash directed intentionally at the linesman in question, nor the subsequent collapse of his game. Mr. Laney did not wish to detract from the excellent play of Ted Wilson, but—

Pam had burrowed back into the *Times*. Jerry finished the account of the semi-finals at Forest Hills, but finished it to himself. They sat in their apartment, a typical American couple, knee deep in Sunday newspapers. Jerry put the sports section aside and regarded his wife. He could guess about where she was.

"How's Reston this morning?" he asked her.

"Wonderful," Pam said. "It's one of the translations of public statements ones. Sssh." Jerry sshed. "Simply marv—Jerry!" Pam said. "Here he is again!"

Jerry ran a hand through his hair.

"Reston?" he said, without much hope. "James Reston?" He did not know that the use of Mr. Reston's given name would bridge this utter gap in relevance. It was worth the try.

"Reston?" Pam repeated. "I just finished Reston. Why would I say he was here again? Why again, I mean?"

"I don't know," Jerry said, keeping it as simple as he could.

"Blanchard," Pam said. "In letters to the editor. The ones they save for Sunday because—listen!"

Jerry listened.

" 'The writer of the following letter, a prominent New York attorney, is widely known as an authority on cats and has written about them extensively,' " Pam read. "At the bottom it's signed 'John Blanchard.' And—"

"Read it," Jerry said. "He certainly does seem to—crop up."

" 'Many readers of the *Times*,' " Pam read, " 'must have been shocked, as I was shocked, by its acceptance of the recently published advertisement of the organization calling itself "The Committee Against Cruelty." Even in its advertising columns, it seems to me and must seem to many, a newspaper of the stature of the

Times owes a responsibility to society as a whole, and is required to consider the public interest.

" 'No one questions the right of Floyd Ackerman, who lists himself as chairman of this "Committee," and others associated with him to hold whatever views they wish on vivisection, and to seek to promulgate them. But what they are doing in this advertisement is, in effect, crying "Fire!" in a crowded theater. It is there, as one of our most distinguished jurists long ago pointed out, that the right of free speech ends.

" 'I refer, of course, to the advertisement's disparaging references to the value of the vaccine which has already done so much to curb infantile paralysis, and this at a time when health authorities are bending every effort to bring about universal inoculation. And this because the development of the vaccine has cost the lives of many monkeys! It is difficult to believe that sentimentality has ever been carried to more dangerous lengths, and that the *Times* has abetted an attitude so essentially immoral.

" 'I cannot, I think, be accused of indifference to animal sufferings. Rather notoriously, I am addicted to cats, and have written a good deal about them. I am a member of several organizations which seek more humane treatment of all our animal friends. But I cannot understand anyone who sets the life of a monkey—yes, or even the life of a cat—above that of a child. I am rather glad I can't.' "

Pam stopped, looked up and awaited comment.

"A little heavy-handed," Jerry said, speaking as an editor. "But rather a nice sting in the tail, I think. Ackerman'll be boiling, if I know Ackerman."

"All right," Pam said, after blinking twice, "do you know Ackerman?"

"Oddly enough," Jerry said. "He brought us a book a while back. 'Criminals in White Coats,' he wanted to call it. Very upset when we said we guessed not. If you're through with the sports section, I'd like to see what Danzig—"

"In due time," Pam said. "Ackerman first."

"Why?"

"Because," Pam said, "all at once everything's full of Mr. Blanchard. I'm beginning to have feelings."

"Not that!" Jerry said. "But, all right. About Ackerman—"

Ackerman had come, in person, to the offices of North Books, Inc., several months before—some time, as Jerry recalled it, in late June. He had come bearing manuscript, a thing which happens even to the best of publishers. He had been—it was to be assumed he still was—a pale and intense man in his middle forties; a very thin man; a man who wore large glasses and, when excited, trembled. He was already excited when, after subterfuge had been exhausted, he was admitted to Jerry's office. He put the manuscript on Jerry's desk and stood on the other side of the desk, shaking with fervor.

"We get all kinds," Jerry told Pam, with resignation. "Ackerman was a bit—excessive. So damned excessive he's a splinter group more or less by himself."

He had, for one thing, suggested that he, then and there, read the book aloud to Gerald North. Jerry had pleaded the pressure of other duties. Ackerman had, then, offered to read sections. He had begun to untie the manuscript—it was loose-paged, and bound with string—and, it seemed to Jerry, his eyes had begun to glitter behind the large glasses.

"Fanatics are one kind," Jerry told Pam. "He is. Vivisection is a sin against the life force, among other things. Research men who perform operations on animals are sadists. They only pretend to seek knowledge; that their goal is the relief of human suffering is a hoax. It's all a conspiracy."

"Goodness," Pam said. "On the other hand, I didn't care for the

wo-headed dog business. Because—what's the use of people having
two heads? And if not—"

Jerry waited politely. Pam did not continue, having made her
point.

"Anyway," Jerry said, "that's it—that was it in about four hundred
yped pages, complete with examples, all of them horrid. Including,
as the advertisement did suggest, as I recall it, that most of the dis-
coveries which have resulted from animal experimentation are
hoaxes too. There were some pictures—I don't know how he laid
hands on them. Very unpleasant pictures."

"None," Pam North said, "of children in iron lungs? Or wheel
chairs?"

That was it, Jerry said. Sentimentality was a vicious thing, Jerry
said. Grant Ackerman was honest—

"Don't," Pam said. "You sound like Mr. Garroway, asking people
f Russians are honest. The people usually look so blank, the poor
hings—so 'so-whatish?' You didn't accept the book?"

"Good God no," Jerry said. "Can I have Danzig now?"

"Did this Mr. Ackerman take that calmly?"

Ackerman had not. The book had been sent back by messenger,
with a note of regret. Mr. Ackerman, shaking more than ever, had
arrived by return mail. "Quicker." He had demanded to see Jerry;
he had said, loudly, that either the book had not been read or that
'they" were paying to have it suppressed. Jerry could hear him in
he reception room, shouting. Jerry had closed his office door.

The last words he had heard, through the closed door, were "I'll
ee about this!"

"It sounds," Pam said, "as if he ought to be locked up somewhere.
But—he's got enough money to get this advertisement printed. And
apparently there are others who feel as strongly. Enough for a committee, anyway." She paused. "I thought," she said, "that that kind
of thing had sort of—died out."

[33]

"Old fanaticisms never die," Jerry said. "Can I have Danzig now?"

"Mr. Blanchard has made another enemy," Pam said, and shuffled papers, seeking the sports section of the *Times*. "He's enemy-prone, isn't he?" She handed Jerry the sports section. "Hmmm," Jerry said. "I'll do the crossword, then," Pam said.

Even that did not distract Gerald North, in whom, each September, the tennis sap rises irresistibly, submerging even his distaste for crossword puzzles.

The next two hours were the uneventful hours of a typical American couple knee deep in Sunday newspapers. It is true that Pam, confronted by a nine-letter word meaning "making white" wrote in the word "blanchard," a little absently, but what are erasers for? It is true that Jerry, reading a review of a novel which had been submitted to and rejected by North Books, Inc., and learning that the reviewer considered it the best work of fiction since *Of Human Bondage,* snorted dangerously. But such things are to be expected in all lives.

IV

SERGEANT ALOYSIUS MULLINS, of Homicide, Manhattan West, was in a somewhat disgruntled mood. Several things irked, one of them being that this looked like turning into a big one—the kind the inspector would ride herd on—and for the moment Mullins was the herd which would be ridden. For the moment and, probably, for some time to come. The captain wouldn't make it for more than an hour at best, since he had to drive down from the country. For another thing, it was Sunday. For still another, everybody around outranked him, and his tongue was sore from saying "sir."

"So you just walked in," Mullins said, to a man with little hair on his head, and bristling gray eyebrows making up for this lack. The man wore a tweed jacket in which red predominated, slacks which were somewhat greenish, and a blue sports shirt without a necktie. "Just walked in and found him dead."

"Dying," the man said. He had told Sergeant Mullins he was Dr. Oscar Gebhardt, which Mullins regarded as a likely story. He had said that death occurred within a few minutes of the time of his arrival.

"And," Mullins said, "you say you came to give what you call rejuvenation shots to a—a *cat*."

It was really the cat part of it which preyed on Mullins's mind. The rest could be endured; would have to be endured. Even saying "sir" to some young squirt from the precinct. But cats were too much. For Sergeant Mullins, cats are always too much. And it sometimes seems to him that he is dogged by cats.

[35]

"How many times?" Dr. Oscar Gebhardt said, and his manner bristled like his eyebrows.

"Mister," Mullins said, "as often as I want you to."

Which was not like Mullins on an ordinary day, and an ordinary case—a case without cats in it. Mullins normally treats the public with the courtesy stipulated in the Manual of Procedure. This is true even when the public wears sports shirts—in the city and on Sunday.

"I," Gebhardt said, "have calls to make. Already I've been held up for—" He looked at his watch. "For almost three hours," he said. "I have an appointment in White Plains at twelve." He looked at his watch again. "Which was an hour ago," he said.

Mullins said that that was too bad, and spoke in a tone without conviction. He said he was afraid the cat in White Plains would have to wait. Or horse or whatever.

Gebhardt sighed deeply. He said he had already explained that he specialized in cats. "Haven't touched a horse in years," he added. "I resent your attitude."

That, also, was too bad. "Once more, from the beginning," Mullins said. "You say it was about ten?"

They were in one of the smaller rooms of an apartment the like of which Mullins had supposed to have vanished from Manhattan, even from the old apartment houses on Riverside Drive. (The smaller room was approximately eighteen feet by twenty, which made it cozy. There were ten rooms in the apartment, all but two of them larger. Why, long ago, the thing hadn't been split up into—)

"Suppose, sergeant, you listen this time," Dr. Gebhardt said. He pointed the index finger of his right hand at Mullins for emphasis. The index finger had a plastic bandage on it. So did the ring finger. There was a somewhat larger bandage on Dr. Gebhardt's left wrist. "You want me to prove all over again who I am? Oscar Gebhardt

[36]

doctor of veterinary surgery. Graduate of Cornell. My office on Park Avenue is at—"

"We'll see," Mullins said. "All you've got to show is a driver's license. You say there are hundreds of people who can identify you —prove you didn't maybe lift the license from somebody. You say that on a Sunday in September most of them would, naturally, be out of town. You say—"

"Sergeant," Gebhardt said, and his voice bristled now. "I listen, even if you don't. I listen to what I say. Don't stand there telling me what I say. Suppose—" He broke off. "All right," he said. "I'm wasting my own time now. It was a few minutes after—"

It had been almost exactly ten o'clock on this Sunday morning when Oscar Gebhardt, D.V.S., had parked his pale yellow Cadillac at the nearest point he could find to the apartment house on Riverside Drive—a building which was now a reminder of the Drive's one-time grandeur. He had walked a block, carrying a small black bag, to the building, which had an enormous lobby. He had walked across the lobby briskly, his heels clicking on marble, to a ridiculously small elevator. On Sunday mornings the elevator was passenger-operated. It was also inclined to stick between floors.

It was a few minutes after ten when the elevator, having hesitated between third and fourth but decided against sticking, stopped at the sixth floor. Dr. Gebhardt was already late by then. He had expected to arrive not later than nine—had, in fact, promised to arrive not later than nine. He had been delayed by an unexpectedly difficult parturition on the part of a Siamese queen. (Inadequate pelvic girdle; should never have been bred; if people had half the sense of cats. To which the answer, somewhat plaintively voiced, had been, "But you should have heard her, doctor.")

He rang the doorbell quickly, three times. This was a habit of which, with no success, he was trying to break himself. He knew that any cat he had treated before went under the nearest object on

[37]

hearing, for a second time, the remembered warning of three quick rings. Which meant that he, and assorted cat owners, spent considerable time under nearest objects, usually beds.

Today, the doorbell was unanswered. Dr. Gebhardt rang again, this time one long ring. Not that that would fool the cats. When there was no response, Dr. Gebhardt fished out of his pocket the key which had been given him for this purpose. ("I won't be there much over the weekend and I'm letting the servants off.") He opened the heavy door and went into the ancient apartment, filled with dark furniture—and an infinity of cat hiding places. It was to be hoped that their owner had remembered to lock the cats up in the kitchen, as he had promised. If not, Amantha would have to skip a shot. Oscar Gebhardt had no intention of pursuing her through ten rooms, with Perkins, the black Manx, and Marigold, the red long-hair, engaging in diversionary tactics.

"He in the habit of giving you the key?" Mullins enquired when Dr. Gebhardt had, for the third time, got to the key. "Mister," Mullins added, to show where he stood on this "doctor" business. Doctors do not go around, especially on Sunday, in oddly assorted garments. They are as neat as their small black bags.

"No. I told you—"

"Had he ever given you a key before?"

"Well," Gebhardt said, "I can't say he had. I explained that." He sighed. "God knows I explained it," he said. "All right—once more. I'm giving one of his cats a series of shots. It's desirable that they be given daily, without interruption. For some reason, he couldn't be sure to be here to let me in—"

"You told me that," Mullins said, unfairly. But he was not in a mood to be fair. Doctor indeed! It was true Gebhardt had produced a small black bag. If he thought that made him look like a doctor. "Go ahead. You went in. Did you yell or anything?"

[38]

"I called out, 'Anybody home?'" Gebhardt said. "If that's what you mean by yelling."

"Nobody answered?"

"Amantha did," Gebhardt said. "Amantha yelled. She's a Siamese. They most always yell."

The Siamese, betrayed by her own vocal responsiveness, had revealed that she was in the rear of the apartment. It had also become pretty evident that she was not in the kitchen, behind a closed door.

The apartment was oddly laid out; it was as if the architect—assuming an architect to have been involved—had, on being confronted with an enormous, roughly square, area said, "Let's put a wall here and another one here and see what happens." What had happened was a corridor in the shape of an inner square, with rooms opening from it on both sides—the outer and more opulent having windows on the street or on a court; the inner rooms (the trapped rooms) having no windows at all, but only air vents. The kitchen was one of the trapped rooms. It was at the rear of the apartment. The corridor provided a race course for cats.

From the foyer, Gebhardt had, he said, gone to his right. Not that it mattered; he could have gone either way. As he passed doors, he opened them and looked inside for cats. The second door he opened was that to a corner room—a library which actually had the appearance of one, being walled with books.

"You figured this—cat—you wanted would be in there? With the door closed? When you had heard her in the rear of the apartment?"

"Sergeant," Gebhardt said, "I never figure where a cat won't be. I never match guesses with a cat. I just look."

"O.K.," Mullins said. "And he was lying on the floor. In about the center of the room."

"He was."

"And not dead?"

"Dying," Gebhardt said.

He was told that he seemed very sure.

"I was," Gebhardt said. "There's not much difference between humans and other animals when it comes to dying."

Aloysius Mullins frowned and started to say something. He remembered he was, after all, a cop. Not, for example, a theologian.

"Did you do anything for him?"

"Made sure. There wasn't anything to be done. Not with his head bashed in the way it was."

"So?"

"Went to find a telephone. There isn't one in the library. As one of your—mob, must have noticed."

Gebhardt had called at twelve minutes after ten, which fitted and which the records verified. He had gone back to the library.

"He was dead then," Gebhardt said. "And if you want to know how I knew, sergeant—he wasn't breathing. When they don't breathe, they're dead."

Oscar Gebhardt was somewhat disgruntled himself. He explained things in the simplest terms, to the simplest, and made no bones about it.

"Usually," Gebhardt added, in the interest of scientific accuracy, but somewhat blunting his point.

He had waited for the police to arrive. He had told a prowl car patrolman what he knew, and told it again to detectives from the precinct and now he had told Mullins three times. It was now twenty minutes after one. Oscar Gebhardt looked pointedly at his watch.

"You'd known him a long time? Since he didn't make anything of letting you have the key?"

"Twenty years," Gebhardt said. "He's had cats for twenty years and I've treated his cats for twenty years. He wrote a book about cats—damned good book—and I gave him some pointers. And I haven't the faintest idea who killed him. And I didn't. He was hit

[40]

one blow, very heavy, with a dull object and it crushed his skull and he died of it. An hour, maybe not more than half an hour, before I found him. His name, in case you haven't found that out, was John Blanchard. He—"

Mullins reddened slightly. He said thanks for nothing, thanks a lot for nothing.

"And," Oscar Gebhardt said, "I've got calls to make. Whether you like cats or not. No use going to White Plains now. But I've got five calls in Manhattan, and one up in the Bronx and two in New Jersey. And if you still think I'm not who I say I am, there are a hundred people—two hundred—right here in Manhattan. Call them up and say you've got a little bald man with eyebrows, wearing funny clothes who says he's Dr. Oscar Gebhardt, a cat specialist. Ask them if they've ever heard he goes around killing people and—"

"Such as?"

"Such as what—oh." Gebhardt paused and his eyebrows quivered. "Good many out of town on a nice weekend like—all right, call some people named North. Mr. and Mrs. Gerald. They just might—"

He stopped, because Mullins's face had changed. It seemed to Oscar Gebhardt, D.V.S., that it had changed for the worse.

***

The telephone bell rang shrilly, unexpectedly. It is unusual for telephone bells to ring in the North apartment at one thirty on Sunday afternoons. Jerry was carrying pre-lunch martinis on a tray and jumped slightly, but managed not to slosh, being a man of experience. Pam looked at him, and was looked at. Then Jerry looked at the tray, with the expression of a man up to his neck in labors. Pam said, "Oh all right, but I don't see why it's always me," and answered the telephone.

"Mrs. North?" a familiar voice said—a voice familiar, but now

[41]

evidently under strain of some sort. Pam said, "Why Sergeant Mullins! Hello."

"There's a man here," Mullins said, "says you know him. A short sort of man sort of bald, with sort of bushy eyebrows. He's got on a red coat and—"

"Of course," Pam said. "Dr. Gebhardt. He always wears a red coat on Sunday. To make it feel like Sunday, because otherwise it's just another—" She stopped herself. "There's a man where, sergeant?" Pam said.

"He found a body," Mullins said. "Says he found a body. Says he's a doctor. That is, cat doctor. Says he came to give reju—" Mullins paused. "Rejuvenation shots," he said with great clarity, but as if he were quoting something preposterous, "to a cat."

"Well," Pam said, "why not? Wait—what body? I mean, whose body?"

"Oh," Mullins said, "man named Blanchard—John Blanchard. But the point is, this man who says he's a vet named Gebhardt says you can identify him. And I guess—"

"I'm sure we can," Pam North said. "We'll come right—where, sergeant?"

"It isn't really nec—"

"Of course it is," Pam said. "How can we tell if we don't see him?"

"Mrs. North," Mullins said, "all I told you was what he looked like and about the coat and right away—"

"Sergeant," Pam said. "How can I really know? Over the telephone. There might be a hundred short bald men wearing reddish sport jackets. Pretending to be—"

"But right off—" Sergeant Mullins said.

"Where?" Pam said.

Mullins hesitated a moment. He accepted the inevitable. He told Pam where.

"As soon as we can," Pam said, and hung up and said, "Jerry!

[42]

Gebby's found a body and it's that Mr. Blanchard of course. And Mullins wants us to come up there and tell him whether it's really Gebby and I knew all along—"

Mutely, Jerry North handed his wife a martini. She took it.

"But we haven't much time," Pam said.

"My dear," Jerry said, "I'm afraid—I'm afraid it's growing on you. Does Mullins really want us in on it? Because you know how—"

"Of course," Pam said. "Didn't he call us?" But she looked at Jerry more carefully, and saw that he was looking at her thoughtfully.

"I know," she said. "But—it isn't as if we could make it not have happened. Because it already has. So when Mullins wants us to say Gebby is Gebby—"

"You know he is," Jerry said. "You said he was right off the bat. Pam—before Mullins gave you his name?"

"Well," Pam said. "Perhaps a little. But—"

"Seeing's believing," Jerry said. "I know, my dear. And one of these days we're going to get us both killed. However—"

Cabs move freely in New York on Sundays. The one the Norths captured moved with somewhat breath-taking freedom. There was a knot of people in front of the old apartment house on Riverside Drive. "Sergeant Mullins wants to see us," Pam told a patrolman, who looked at them somewhat stonily. Jerry thought that this was the overstatement of the decade, or, at any rate, of the day. But they were sent along to Mullins—to Mullins, and Dr. Oscar Gebhardt, to whom Pam said, "Hello, Gebby."

"Took you long enough," Gebhardt said, to her. "Well?" he said to Mullins.

Mullins guessed so. They could get in touch with Gebhardt if the need arose.

"Obviously," Gebhardt said. "Use the telephone."

He got his black bag; he went out of the room.

"Well," Mullins said. "Thanks Mrs. North. Mr. North. It was

good of you to come up. I'll tell the loot—that is, the captain—when he gets here. So I don't know as there's any reason for you—"

"Sergeant Mullins," Pam North said. "We knew Mr. Blanchard was going to be killed."

Mullins looked at her and slowly his mouth opened. Jerry looked at her. He ran the fingers of his right hand through his hair.

"Well," Pam said, "almost. Because—"

"Because what, Pam?" Captain William Weigand, of Homicide, Manhattan West, said from the doorway. "And don't you think you should have mentioned it?"

"An indignant tennis player, for one thing," Pam North said. "And—"

She was interrupted. A Siamese cat came around Bill Weigand at a brisk trot, now and then looking back anxiously over her shoulder. The room they were in had been, evidently, Blanchard's office. It contained a large desk, and leather chairs, and a leather sofa.

"Stop her, somebody!" Dr. Oscar Gebhardt said, testily, with contempt for inefficiency, from outside. He trotted into the room after the Siamese cat, holding a hypodermic syringe in one hand. The cat, after one more quick backward glance, went under the sofa. "Damn," Gebhardt said. "Four of you, and you couldn't stop one cat. Here, Amantha. Nice kitty. Pretty kitty." Oscar Gebhardt spoke words of endearment in a tone of consuming anger.

"Mrr—ow-aough," Amantha said, at some length, from under the couch.

"Close the door, somebody," Gebhardt said. Bill Weigand kicked the door closed. "And move the damned sofa," Gebhardt said, to nobody in particular. Mullins looked at him. "You," Gebhardt said. "Big enough, aren't you? And this is sterile." He waved the syringe. "Put it down and I'll have to boil it again." Mullins stared at him.

"Come on, Mullins," Jerry said, and went to the sofa and began to pull at one end of it. Mullins stared briefly at Jerry North. He

[44]

went to the other end of the sofa and pulled. It was a heavy sofa, but it moved. The trouble was that Amantha moved under it.

"Farther out," Pam said, and, when it was far enough out, went behind the sofa. She lay down on the floor and reached an arm under the sofa. "Nice Amantha," Pam North said, in the tone of a coo. "Pretty Amantha."

"Yow-ow-wohr—*uh*," Amantha said. "WOW!"

"Such a way to talk!" Pam said. "Ouch!"

"Bad?" Gebhardt enquired, with more politeness than interest.

"Nick," Pam said. "Sergeant. She's at your end. I'm pushing and—"

Amantha came out. Her ears were laid back. She paused briefly to hiss and went across the room and under a chair.

"Why didn't you grab her, for God's sake?" Gebhardt said to Mullins. "Went right through your hands." He waved the hypodermic at Mullins.

"Listen," Mullins said. "If you think—"

"Move the chair, sergeant," Bill Weigand said. "I'll catch her if she comes this way. Pam?"

"Coming out," Pam said, and came out from behind the sofa, and brushed herself. "I do think, sergeant—" she began, but did not finish. She went to one side of the chair and got down on her knees beside it. "Nice kitty," Pam said. "You ornery little beast." She said the last in dulcet tones.

Amantha said nothing whatever.

Mullins looked around somewhat wildly. Then he got down on his knees in front of the chair, which was large and low. Jerry knelt opposite his wife; Bill Weigand went behind the chair and also knelt. Gebhardt remained near the door, holding the syringe like a baton.

"You look like a prayer meeting," Gebhardt said, with some pleasure. "Or a crap game."

[45]

"Push," Bill said, over the chair, to Mullins. Mullins pushed.

"WOW—OW!" Amantha said, and the moving chair exposed her. She tried to back under.

"*Grab her!*" Gebhardt shouted and started forward. And Mullins grabbed the little café-au-lait cat, with brown ears and face and legs, and long brown tail. He held her dangling.

"Desk," Gebhardt said. "Hold her down."

Mullins looked around somewhat wildly, Amantha dangling. He held the cat out toward Pam.

"*Desk!*" Gebhardt said. "How many times—"

Mullins put the little cat down on the desk top.

"Push her down hard," Gebhardt said. "Front end. Good and hard. They're tougher than they look."

"Good God," Mullins said, but he pressed down on the little cat's shoulders. She glared up at him from wide blue eyes.

"Don't let go until I say," Gebhardt said, and was around the cat. He rubbed her flank with a dab of cotton which he had carried with the syringe. He pushed the needle in, and the little cat was a spring of rage under Mullins's big hands. She twisted. She screamed. Gebhardt pressed the plunger. Amantha was a tortured cat. She mentioned it.

"*Let her go!*" Gebhardt said, loudly. "*Quick, man!*"

Mullins yanked his hands up.

Amantha was a released spring. She paused only long enough—and it did not seem she really paused at all—to rake Mullins's right thumb with a needle tooth. She then went back under the sofa.

"Good," Gebhardt said. "Not much trouble after all. Get you, sergeant?"

Mullins shook blood from his hand. Not much blood, to be sure. But blood. He glared at Gebhardt.

"Have to move fast," Gebhardt said. "Even when they're getting

[46]

along, as she is, they're pretty quick. Fortunately, she's a sweet-tempered little thing. Aren't you, Amantha?"

The cat answered from under the sofa. She said, "mrr—ough," but with no special violence.

"Knows it's over for the day," Gebhardt said. "Well, got to be getting along. I'd put a little iodine on that, sergeant." He did not, it occurred to Pam, speak in tones of much sympathy. "Never got a really bad infection myself, but now and then— As I said, you've got to be firm with them. Firm and fast."

He nodded, confirming his own statement. He went out of the room again.

Mullins prepared to speak.

"As a matter of fact, sergeant," Pam North said, "you didn't need us, you know. All you had to do was to look at Gebby's hands. Bandages. Anybody could tell he's a cat vet." She looked at Mullins and shook her head. "A matter of deduction," Pam said. "Obvious, my dear sergeant."

For a moment the glare remained in the eyes of Sergeant Aloysius Mullins. They waited. The glare faded and Mullins slowly, widely, began to grin. Mullins's face is large, but the grin fitted it.

"O.K.," Mullins said. "O.K. the bunch of you."

V

THEY WAITED in their apartment for Captain William Weigand, Sergeant Aloysius Mullins. They had been told to go there; told to wait there. If they didn't mind. While spadework was done. "We'll be along," Bill told them. "To hear how come you knew Blanchard was going to be killed."

"If we didn't mind indeed," Pam said to Jerry, as they waited. They had waited first with sandwiches, in lieu of lunch. They waited then, for some time, with conversation—with some attempt to determine what, if anything, they did have to tell the men from homicide they had known so long.

"A woman with fringe," Pam said. "An injured tennis player. A man who's fanatic about vivisection. You'd have thought he was killing Amantha, wouldn't you? And really it's no more than a prick."

"Tell them that," Jerry said. "I must say, however, Amantha doesn't seem to need much rejuvenating."

"Poor Mullins," Pam said, and reverted. She said that it didn't, did it, seem like so much when you listed it. A woman with fringe, a blond youth with a temper, a middle-aged man with a fixation.

"Perhaps," Pam said, "I went too far. We didn't know he was going to be killed. Only that he was enemy-prone. And, of course, inclined to sit in judgment."

They didn't, Jerry agreed, actually know much about the late John Blanchard. Bill would know more.

"We've got stamps to give," Pam said and, when Jerry raised eyebrows, added, "Trading."

"On the other hand," Jerry said, "we could sit this one out."

"We always could have," Pam said. "Except the very first one. We never have. Every time, it seemed there were circumstances. Speaking of time, isn't it about?"

Jerry looked at his watch. It was ten minutes past six.

"It is indeed," Jerry said, and got up, and moved quickly—moved to the kitchen and the refrigerator, to the bar in the living room. Ice made pleasant sounds in a shaker. "We're creatures of habit," Pam said, accepting. "How nice for us."

One of their habits is to drink slowly. They had not finished their first, not quite finished, when the doorbell rang at a few minutes before seven. Bill came in and Mullins followed him, and Bill said, "Phew!" Jerry mixed again, this time three in the shaker, a solitary old-fashioned. (Without fruit salad; Mullins was being reformed.) Mullins had a small bandage on his right thumb.

"Right," Bill Weigand said, after a sip. "Now—give."

They gave—gave a woman in fringe at a cat show, the identification of Blanchard by a woman who ran what Pam called a cat store; gave an indignant tennis player.

"Which last," Jerry said, "was in the papers. Except, not the affair in the garden bar."

"This Mears," Bill said. "He was really sore? All-out sore? About calls in a tennis match?"

Mullins emphasized scepticism by shaking his head slowly.

Apparently there was an angle, Jerry said—an angle which included money. As Al Laney had implied—a question of an offer for a professional tour. Whether Doug Mears needed money—Jerry shrugged. He said that a good many of them did; that amateur tennis, although it would be absurd to contend that it did not pay—to a degree by subterfuge—had in recent years become an apprenticeship to a profession. About Mears— He shrugged again.

"Also," Pam said, "the girl's in it somehow. A pretty girl with red

[49]

hair. Not dyed, I don't think. At the table with Mr. Blanchard and Mr. Mears—looked at her."

This was amplified. Bill Weigand said, "Ummm."

"We haven't got too much on Blanchard yet," he said. "He was fifty-seven, according to *Who's Who*. A widower. Childless, apparently. An attorney by profession, but not in active practice for a long time. If any time. Didn't need to be, I gather, having enough of what it takes."

Blanchard had been a widower for some fifteen years, living alone, with two servants, in the old-fashioned apartment which had been his parents'. It had been a "good" address those many years ago; it no longer was; it was evident that Blanchard had not minded.

"Perhaps," Pam said, "he felt that his living there *made* it a good address." They regarded her. "He looked like that," Pam said.

Admittedly, this was possible. It did not, at the moment, seem to have much importance. Except that it might, if Pam was right, give them some measure of the dead man. It is always desirable to measure the violently dead; it is seldom easy. Measurement of the late John Blanchard was proceeding slowly. Partly, this was due to the fact that the day was Sunday, when it is difficult to find out anything about anything. People who might have answers to questions which might be asked are, generally, inaccessible. Offices are closed; bank vaults, including those which shelter safe-deposit boxes, are sealed inexorably by time as well as by heavy locks.

The apartment had, so far, yielded only bits and pieces.

When Dr. Oscar Gebhardt had found Blanchard, the attorney—and judge of cats and the fall of white balls on the worn grass of tennis courts—had been dying alone in his apartment. If one did not count three cats. He might have been struck down minutes before Gebhardt found him or, conceivably, two hours before. He had been struck in the back of the head with a heavy object, a blunt object; an object with a dull point.

[50]

"They say," Bill told the Norths, "that the wound was the sort that might have been made if he'd been knocked backward against the corner of a desk. Or of a desk drawer. Only—he would have had to hit it very violently. Been thrown against it. And there are no other marks of violence on the body. Gebhardt was right, incidentally, in thinking there was nothing anybody could have done by the time he got there. Whole back of the skull bashed in. Brain laceration."

Blanchard had been dressed in slacks and jacket and rubber-soled suède shoes. He had made himself coffee that morning; a little coffee remained in a Chemex and it was still faintly warm when the police arrived. Tasted, it had seemed reasonably fresh. He had fed the cats, who, apparently, ate from a single dish. He had fed them chopped beef, jarred for small children; a little remained and had not dried out. Precisely when he had done these things there was no way of determining.

The two servants Gebhardt had mentioned were a man and wife; two of the rooms of the apartment had been their bedroom and sitting room; one of the baths their bath. The man was quite tall and thin; the woman short and decidedly plump. The clothes in their closet revealed this. There was nothing to indicate where they had gone. They were Mr. and Mrs. Robert Sandys, or had received mail so addressed, and dropped envelopes into a wastepaper basket. There was nothing in their rooms to indicate that they did not intend to return.

Blanchard had owned two cars—a 1957 Buick sedan; a later model Cadillac. The Cadillac was in a garage three blocks away; the Buick was not. Sandys had picked it up Saturday morning and it had not been returned.

The most likely thing was that Blanchard had given the Sandyses the weekend off, and the use of the Buick to enjoy it in. They might be anywhere.

[51]

"Looking at leaves," Pam said. "Only it will be early unless they go way up."

Looking at, or for, leaves was a possibility. There were dozens of other possibilities. If the Sandyses did not return within reasonable time—that evening would seem a reasonable time—they would be looked for. They would be able to help the police in the measuring of a man killed.

In the apartment in the old building, John Blanchard had been, in a way, more isolated than if he had lived in a big country house, miles from anywhere, deep in many acres. Such houses are approached by car; cars are seen, perhaps speculated about.

At any time, but particularly on a Sunday morning, anyone might turn off the sidewalk into the apartment house Blanchard had lived in and been unnoticed, unremarked. After noon on weekdays, but only after three in the afternoon on Sundays, the small elevators which served the two wings of the building were attended; at other hours they were passenger-operated.

Anyone could walk across an empty lobby, as Gebhardt said he had walked, and gone into an elevator and pressed a proper button and been seen by nobody. From the small lobby on the sixth floor, two doors opened—one to Blanchard's apartment and the other to a presumably similar apartment occupied by people named Butler. The Butlers had left the previous Friday on a cruise.

Whoever had killed Blanchard had been let in by Blanchard. Or had had a key of his own. Or her own.

Pam North raised eyebrows at the last qualification.

"Right," Bill said. "Depending on what was used, of course. And on the strength of the lady. But at the spot hit the skull isn't very—resistant. Blanchard's wasn't, anyway."

They hadn't, Jerry gathered, found what had been used. He assumed the theory wasn't that Blanchard had been hit in the back of the head with a desk? With the corner of a desk?

[52]

"Jerry!" Pam said. "Nobody could hit anybody with a desk. A table, perhaps, but—" She stopped, abruptly. "Bill!" she said. "Scratching post?"

Bill Weigand blinked for a moment. But then he stopped blinking and his eyes narrowed thoughtfully. He said, "Hmmmm."

"You may well," Pam said. "Wait."

She went out of the living room and shortly, from some distance, there was a sound of banging. "We put it out of sight," Jerry said. "Because—well, just because."

"I know," Bill said. "Because she—"

"Both of us," Jerry said.

Pam came back, with her hands full. "I wish," she said, "you'd find someplace else to put our rackets. Both of them fell off and one came down on my toe and—" She stopped. "Anyway," she said, and waved what her hands were full of—waved it a little truculently, but obviously in demonstration.

It was a square post, about three feet long, set into a broad square base of polished wood. The post was covered with a carpet-like material, in this instance somewhat tattered. It was most tattered at the height a medium-sized cat might reach when the feline urge to scratch came upon him.

Pam raised the post above her head and held it so that, if brought down violently—on, for example, another head—the corner of the squared base would strike first. She held it so for some seconds. She said, "Well? He had one?"

Bill Weigand nodded his head. He said, "Right, Pam."

Sergeant Mullins got up and took the cat-scratching post from Pam and hefted it and examined the joint between post and base. He put it down and said, "Might break off, maybe. But, on the other hand, maybe not. He had three of um. One for each cat, I guess." He looked at Weigand. "Maybe?" he said.

"Right," Bill said. "By all means, Mullins."

Mullins went to the telephone in the living room. He dialed and waited.

He said, "Nate?" and then, "Know what a scratching post looks like?" He waited again, momentarily. "That's it," he said. "For cats. There's three of them up there and it looks like it could be—"

Briefly, he told Nate what it looked like it could be. "So maybe—" he said, and stopped.

He said, "Oh," in a slightly diminished tone. He said, "O.K., Nate." He put his hand over the receiver and turned to Bill Weigand. "Nate Shapiro," he said. "Thought of it. Sent them along to the lab. Anything else—yeah, Nate?"

Again he listened. He said, "Maybe you'd better talk to the loot, Nate. I mean the captain."

Weigand put down an empty glass, after glancing at it briefly. He crossed the room and took the telephone from Mullins and said, "Yes, Shapiro?" He listened. He said, "Ummm." He said, "Right." He said, "Did she? That's interesting." He said, "Right. We'll come back—" and stopped and turned and looked, briefly, at the Norths. He said, into the telephone, "Tell you what, Nate. Have one of the boys bring her down here. Right? All informal like. And only if she doesn't mind coming. You know the pitch." He listened again. "By all means in her own car, if she'd rather. Somebody along to help her park, don't you think?" He listened again, briefly, said "Right," once more and put the telephone back in its cradle.

"A young woman walked into the apartment," Bill told them. "Started to, anyway. Had a key to it. Said Mr. Blanchard had invited her to drop by for a drink. Very much upset to find out that he'd had his last."

"So," Jerry said, "she's being brought here. To the North station house." He went to make drinks.

"Well," Bill said, and sat down and waited. "There's one other

[54]

point. Seems she's got red hair. Very pretty red hair, Nate Shapiro says. In that mournful way of his."

Jerry distributed drinks. When he put Pam's down by her chair he said, "Sorry about the foot," and was looked at, momentarily, without apparent comprehension. Then Pam said, "Oh, that. I'd forgotten." She lifted one foot and looked at it. "Seems all right," she said. "It was just at the moment it—" She stopped, since she was clearly not being listened to.

Gerald North said that he'd be damned and went off down the hall toward the closet from which Pam had brought the scratching post—the, sadly, no longer used scratching post. There was, again, some rattling from the closet. Then Jerry came back. Just inside the living room he paused and then held, above his head, a sheathed tennis racket. He held it as if he were about to make an overhead smash.

The racket was in a cover. It was also in a wooden press—an oblong arrangement of wood, with turnbolts at each corner, clamping the racket.

When he had full attention, Jerry brought the racket sweeping down, hard—and so that one of the wooden corners of the press, rather than the face of the racket, would strike anything that intervened.

"Pretty much like the corner of a desk, isn't it?" Jerry said, and patted the corner of the racket press with what appeared to be affection. "A good deal easier to handle than a desk, too. Good and heavy in the head a racket is, when there's a press on it."

Bill Weigand put his drink down and held his hand out. Jerry put the racket in it, and Bill swung it slowly back and forth.

"Quite heavy," he said, and handed it to Mullins, who stood up and swung it as if it were a club. "What d'yuh know?" Mullins asked himself.

"Blanchard used to be quite a tennis player," Jerry said. "Probably had a few rackets still around in the apartment. Nobody throws rackets away. Always figures that sometime he'll get back to it. Never quite gives up." He looked at the racket Mullins held as one might look at a stranger. "Probably warped by now," he said. "Strings gone, probably." He went back to his drink.

Weigand nodded to Mullins, who went again to the telephone, and dialed again, and again said, "Nate?" He listened briefly. He said, "O.K. I'll tell the loot-I-mean-captain. But there's another thing, Nate. See if Blanchard had any tennis rackets lying around, huh? In—" He turned and looked toward the others for enlightenment. "Presses," Jerry said.

"Presses," Sergeant Mullins said, to Detective Nathan Shapiro, supervising further investigations in the outsize apartment on Riverside Drive. "Wood gadgets that clamp—oh." He listened. He said, "Yeah, Nate. That was the idea. Be seeing." He hung up.

"Two rackets," he said. "Both in presses." Weigand raised eyebrows. "Yeah," Mullins said. "Nate's sent them along to the lab. Also, the girl's on her way down."

They sipped, seated again, the racket on the floor by Sergeant Mullins's chair.

"Only," Pam North said, after some minutes, "it's a little hard to picture. Somebody walks in and says, 'By the way, Mr. Blanchard, have you got a tennis racket handy? Like to brain you with it, if you have.' And Blanchard says—"

She did not finish her sentence. She finished her drink, instead.

"It seems stronger than usual," she said. "Did you put in extra vermouth, Jerry?"

VI

HILDA LATHAM was slender, even in a green woolen suit. Her eyes were greenish-blue, and she was very pretty. And she had dark red hair. When the precinct man who had come down with her said, at the doorway, "This is Miss Latham, captain," and, without being told, went out again and closed the door behind him, Bill Weigand looked quickly at Pam North. Quickly, just perceptibly, Pam nodded.

"Nice of you to come down, Miss Latham," Bill said, and Pam said, for herself and Jerry, that they were the Norths and could they get Miss Latham something to drink? The girl shook her head. There was a tightness about her curving lips; there was, Pam thought, a wariness in her greenish eyes. But it's quite likely, Pam told herself, that I'm seeing what I look for.

"I want to do anything," Hilda Latham said. Her voice was soft, yet very clear. "Anything I can. Only I don't—" She did sit down, then. "It's so hard to believe," she said, and this time the soft clear voice trembled a little. "When the men told me—" She did not continue. She looked from one to the other.

They appreciated her coming down, Bill told her again. He didn't know, either, what she could tell them. Except that it might help them to talk to anyone who had known John Blanchard well, as he assumed—

"All my life, nearly," Hilda Latham said, and her soft voice was steady again. "Since I was a little girl, anyway. He and father had been friends for years. And for a couple of years—no, three years—he and Aunt Susan—" She paused. She smiled faintly. The smile

[57]

was without meaning. "I'm not keeping things very straight, am I?" she said. "Aunt Susan was Mrs. Blanchard. She died years ago. Not my aunt, really. Just—just a word a child uses. You know?"

"Of course he does," Pam said. "Won't you change your mind about a drink, Miss Latham? Probably you could do with one."

"Well—" the red-haired girl said, and again arranged a smile on curved lips—a smile for convention's sake. "Anything."

A martini would be all right; a martini would be fine.

There was nothing, there had been nothing, to indicate that Hilda Latham remembered the Norths as among those who had watched the short, bitter scene in the garden bar at Forest Hills. There was no reason she should remember. She, not they, had been at the center, been the watched.

"Thank you," she said, to Jerry, for the drink. "You'll wonder how I happened to have a key to John's apartment."

"Aunt" Susan, but not "Uncle" John. But those appellations would have died with childhood. The girl was—what? In her quite early twenties, probably.

"Anything you can tell us," Bill Weigand said. "About the key, then?"

Since her father—"Graham Latham?" She looked from one to the other, apparently for some sign that the name was recognized. She got none. Anyway—

When her father had retired, about five years before, they had given up the apartment they had in Manhattan, and now lived all year around in the Southampton house. She had started to say, now did say, that there, in Southampton, before Mrs. Blanchard died, the Blanchards had had a house "next door." Anyway—

Her father and mother came into New York infrequently. Now and then, for a week or two in the winter, they came in and stayed at a hotel and went to the theater. But she came in much more frequently and when she did usually stayed in John Blanchard's apartment. The key was so that she could come and go when she wished, whether he was there or not.

"There's room there for half a dozen," Hilda said. "I could just pop in, and not even bother him. Just tell Mrs. Sandys—" She broke off. "They weren't there today?" she said. "The Sandyses?"

"No," Bill told her. "Apparently they had the weekend off."

"Because of the tournament," Hilda said, and nodded her head so that the deep red hair swirled around her face. "He'd be there—" Again she broke off. "Would have expected to be there," she said, "most of the weekend. Umpiring—filling in on the lines. It's hard to find linesmen sometimes and—"

She shrugged slim shoulders, suggesting that she had wandered far from anything which would be found interesting, which would help. "Anyway," she said, "that's why he let Mr. and Mrs. Sandys off, I expect. If they'd been there—was it somebody who broke in? A burglar?"

"Conceivably," Bill said. "Only—the door wasn't forced. And, nothing was disturbed. There's nothing to indicate that Mr. Blanchard surprised somebody ransacking the apartment. You just happened to be in town today, Miss Latham? Or were you in last night? Stay at the apartment?"

She hesitated for a moment. Then she shook her head, and again the red hair swirled.

"No," she said. "I came to see if John was—all right. I was home last night. Most of this morning."

They waited.

"I was going to have lunch with him," she said. "At the inn at Forest Hills. I drove in from Southampton to have lunch with him. He—he didn't come. I tried to get him on the telephone and then —then asked people at the club. He'd been going to umpire a mixed doubles match and hadn't showed up there, either. I tried again a couple of times on the phone and then watched the finals—the men's finals. Then—well, then I drove in to see if he was all right. I said he'd asked me to come in for a drink but that was—just something to say. The first thing that came into my mind."

That didn't matter, Bill Weigand told her. Had she any particular reason to worry about John Blanchard?

She was quick on that. He'd invited her to lunch. He had agreed to umpire a match. He had kept neither appointment. Which was unlike him.

It was only that? Nothing more specific?

Greenish-blue eyes went very wide open. Specific? What did Captain Weigand mean, specific?

"I don't know," Bill said. "Were you afraid he'd been taken suddenly ill? A heart attack—something like that?"

"I didn't know what to think," she said. "Of course— I've said I was worried. That that's why I came in. When nobody answered the telephone—not John or Sandys or anybody—of course I was worried. John isn't—I mean wasn't—a young man."

"But a healthy man? So far as you knew?"

"Completely. So far as I knew. As he ever said."

"You saw a good deal of him?"

"Not a good deal, really. I'd stay over at the apartment—oh, perhaps once every two weeks. Oftener in the winter. Now and then he'd spend a weekend with us. He was daddy's friend, really. And mother's."

She didn't, she told them, know much about John Blanchard's other friends, associates. "Of course, he was a lot older." She knew of his interest in cats; she supposed he knew a good many people who also were interested in cats—as breeders, showers of cats. About them, she knew nothing. He was a member of the West Side Tennis Club, and still played now and then. She played there too, now and then. She wasn't good—not really good. She'd found out "years" ago she wasn't going to be. Her father was a member of the club.

She supposed that John Blanchard had known a lot of people through his interest in tennis, his membership in the umpires' association. A good many of the men he probably knew she knew by name; some to smile at, nod to. Of course, most of them were older. "His age."

A friend of the family—that was the picture. A much older man; a man like an uncle; a man who let her stay when she liked in an apartment too large for one man. She had been fond of him; very fond of him—as a pretty young woman may be fond of a man like an elderly uncle. That he should have been—*killed!* Who would want—?

They were trying to find that out; that was what it was all about. She couldn't help there? Blanchard had said nothing to her which now, in the light of what had happened, took on meaning—meaning it had not had when he said it?

She shook her head, the red hair swaying about her pretty face.

He had not spoken of anyone with whom he had had—call it a disagreement? Had not seemed worried when she saw him last?

Again the head shook, the hair swayed.

She had had her chance; had not taken it. Bill Weigand's tone was just perceptibly different on the next question.

"Miss Latham," he said, "you haven't mentioned the incident at Forest Hills yesterday. In the garden bar. You don't think that was germane to what I asked?"

Her eyes widened at that; their expression changed momentarily. "How did—" she began, and caught herself. "Oh," she said, "that." Her tone dismissed "that."

"That was nothing. Doug Mears sort of—flies off the handle, as daddy says. I'm sure he was sorry right away afterward. Probably apologized. In matches the boys—and the girls too, sometimes—get so keyed up that—" She stopped. "It didn't mean anything," she said.

"It never occurred to me that you would think it was—what you said. Germane. Just an excited kid."

"Mears is—what, Jerry?"

"Twenty-four," Jerry said. "About that. Twenty-three or twenty-four."

"Just a kid, anyway," the girl said. "Younger than you make it sound. A tennis-playing kid."

"A friend of yours, Miss Latham?"

"Not especially. I know a good many of them—the tennis-playing kids and—"

"Miss Latham," Bill said, "more or less by accident, we've learned quite a bit about this—incident. You spoke to Mears as if you knew him rather well. As if you were—cautioning him. And Mears said something about—" He looked at Pam North. She hesitated.

"All right," she said. "My husband and I happened to be there, Miss Latham. Mr. Mears said something about Mr. Blanchard's having got what he wanted and then—" Pam closed her eyes; concentrated. She opened them.

"That it was—was sitting right there," she said. "Wasn't that it, Jerry? About it? And—you were sitting there with Mr. Blanchard, you know. It sounded as if—"

"No," the girl said, and spoke quickly. "There wasn't anything like that. I don't know why you say—I was a little embarrassed, because all at once everybody was looking at us and—there wasn't anything like that."

Pam looked at Jerry.

"That's the way I remember it," Jerry said. "You said 'Doug' a couple of times as if—as if you were asking him to—call it behave himself. As if how he behaved concerned you."

"Doug Mears?" she said, in apparent astonishment. "Why on earth should what he does—oh, I didn't want to be part of a scene. Nobody does. Perhaps I did say something to—to stop him. Said

[62]

'Oh, *Doug*' the way one does, meaning—" She stopped again. She looked at Bill Weigand. "That was all," she said. "If Doug said anything about John's having what he wanted I don't know what he meant. And, I don't remember anything like—"

The doorbell rang. Jerry went to the door. Two men were outside it—a rangy young man, hatless, with blond short hair; a heavier and somewhat older man, who wore a hat.

"Compliments of Detective Shapiro," the heavier man said. "A Mr. Doug Mears. Showed up at the apartment, Shapiro says, and—"

"Hildy!" Doug Mears said. "What the hell are you—" He did not finish. When he first saw the girl, Pam thought, there had been light in his face. The light went out.

"Come in, Mr. Mears," Bill Weigand said. "We were just talking about you."

Mears hesitated.

"I'd do what the captain says, Mr. Mears," the heavy man said. "Hiya, Al."

Mullins had moved closer to the door. He looked very large. He said, "Hiya, Jimmy? How's tricks?" but not as if either remark were a question, requiring an answer.

Mears came in. He stood in the room as the heavy man closed the door on them.

"What about me?" Mears said. He didn't look particularly like a kid. His face was young enough. His expression was not. He spoke, not to Bill Weigand, or to Mullins or the Norths. He spoke to Hilda Latham. "You've been doing the talking, Hildy?"

"Nothing," she said. "They've got some crazy idea. I was just—just telling them how crazy—"

Mears did not wait for her to finish. He looked now at the others. He said, "What kind of a deal is this, anyway? Seems to me I'm being pushed around. What's the idea?"

"Not pushed," Bill Weigand said, and spoke pleasantly, without

[63]

insistence, without rancor. "I'm a police captain. Investigating a murder. John Blanchard's murder. This is a police sergeant. Mr. and Mrs. North are—friends of mine. Things happened to work out so that—" He paused; momentarily he blinked. When he told Deputy Chief Inspector Artemus O'Malley how things had "happened" to work out— And, until that moment, the course of events had seemed so natural. Momentarily, in his mind, Bill listened to the explosion of Deputy Chief Inspector Artemus O'Malley.

"You don't need to say anything unless you want to," he said, mildly, to the tall, the rangy—and most obviously the angry—tennis player.

"You're damned right," Mears said.

"Only," Bill said, "I could take you in for questioning. To a station house. Even hold you for a while as a material witness. You could have a lawyer and—"

"What's she been telling you?" Mears said.

"Nothing," Hilda Latham said. "Nothing, Doug. Because there's nothing—"

"You're damned right there isn't," Mears said. He was, evidently, a man who did not wait for the obvious to be completed. "Johnny Blanchard said to drop around for a drink if I was going to be in town this afternoon and when I get there—"

"Doug," the girl said. "They do know about yesterday. Not only what was in the papers. Somehow—these people—" She indicated the Norths. "They happened to be having a drink when—"

"So what?" Mears said. He looked now at Bill Weigand. "You don't for God's sake want to try to make anything out of that?" He looked at Hilda Latham. "And you," he said. "Are a sweetheart. Really and truly a sweetheart." His tone was bitter.

"Miss Latham," Bill Weigand said, without emphasis, "also has told us there is nothing to be made out of that. If there isn't, we won't make anything. When you went around for a drink, you didn't know Mr. Blanchard was dead?"

[64]

"That," Mears said, "is a hell of a damned fool question. If I knew he was dead, how the hell'd I think he could give me a drink?"

"Bill," Pam North said, "he's really got something there, hasn't he? What would you like to drink, Mr. Mears? Or are you in training or something?"

Mears stared at her for a moment.

"Because," Pam said, "all the rest of us are." She looked around at the glasses. "Were," she corrected. "If you don't drink we've probably got some—"

"Two hours ago," Mears said, "Nellie and I lost the silliest damn match you ever— So." He looked around again. "This is the damnedest setup," he said. "Scotch, if it's handy."

And he looked around for a chair. It appeared that Mr. Doug Mears had decided to play along. When Jerry had made his rounds, Mears did, to a degree, play along. Now and then, his tone sharpened, his ever-ready temper showed through. But as an exasperated young man, and one who had had a disappointing tournament, he seemed to be doing what he could to play along.

He did not deny that he had been sore as hell at John Blanchard. But he pointed out that that was yesterday. So, he'd made a fool of himself. It wasn't the first time. "I needed that match," he said. "Might have made a hell of a lot of difference. Water under the bridge, now."

He'd calmed down after the scene in the garden bar. Toward evening he had run into John Blanchard at the Forest Hills Inn and apologized. They could prove that, if they wanted to. Plenty of people had heard him.

What had he meant, Blanchard had got "what he wanted?"

How did he know? He was sore. He'd said the first thing that came into his head. He supposed—got him beaten. It was a damn silly thing to say.

About what Blanchard had wanted being seated at the table?

"Don't remember anything like that," Mears said. And if he

looked at Hilda Latham quickly, was not looked at, looked away again, what did that mean? The question was Pam North's, to herself. He had to look at somebody. Hilda Latham was a rewarding somebody to look at.

It had been during his meeting at the inn, during his apology, that John Blanchard had invited him to drop by the next afternoon —this afternoon—for a drink? If he happened to be in town?

"Yes," Mears said. "Sure. I said I still didn't get the foot-fault business, and what was I doing wrong? He said, drop by and he'd try to explain. He was with some other people then and I was meeting a couple of guys myself. So—"

So, having been eliminated from the mixed doubles early in the afternoon, having watched the finals of the men's singles—the Australian had won, in straight sets, to nobody's surprise—Doug Mears had driven into town, and up to the apartment in Riverside Drive. He had rung the doorbell and—

"Things sort of blew up in my face."

He guessed that, when he had first come into the apartment, this apartment, he had blown up himself. O.K., he'd said he did sometimes. O.K., he was sorry.

He said this to everybody. He looked at Hilda Latham. This time, briefly, she looked at him. Her expression didn't, to the watching Pamela North, reveal anything. My intuition must be slipping, Pam thought.

So?

Where had he been at, say, around nine that morning?

He flared briefly at that. What the hell—? O.K. He had been at the inn at Forest Hills. He'd either been just getting up, or eating breakfast, having just got up. Alone? So far as he remembered, he hadn't seen anybody he knew. So?

That was about all, for the moment, Bill told him, told Hilda Latham. Mears stood up; the girl did not.

"Come on, Hildy," Mears said. "Unless you've moved in here?"

She hesitated.

"For God's sake," Mears said, with impatience. "For God's sake, come *on!*"

She stood up, then. She said, "I—"

The telephone rang. Jerry looked at it with reproach. "One of you," he said, and Mullins answered. But it was Bill Weigand who spoke to Nathan Shapiro, on Riverside Drive, and a long, long way from Brooklyn. Bill said, "Yes, Nate?"

"Another one's showed up," Nathan Shapiro said, deep depression in his voice. "Guy named Ackerman. Starey-eyed sort of man. Teddy opened the door and he said, 'Where's this man Blanchard?' sort of as if he'd come to shoot him. So do you want we should send him down too or—"

"No," Bill said. "I'll come up, Nate. Put Mr. Ackerman in storage for now."

He hung up. He told Hilda Latham and the tall tennis player that he hoped they wouldn't get lost, not go too far away. They both, a little unexpectedly but most politely, thanked Mr. and Mrs. North for the drinks, and for a moment it appeared that Hilda might go further, might thank them for such a nice party. "Come *on,*" Mears said, and they went on.

"Did you say Ackerman?" Jerry said, and then explained Ackerman. Bill said, "Well—well."

"Will Kleenex be all right?" Pam asked, and Bill said it would do, and they wrapped in tissue, carefully, the cocktail glass Hilda Latham had used, the highball glass from which Mears had drunk.

"So nice you could drop in," Pamela North said, as William Weigand and Sergeant Mullins dropped out, taking wrapped glasses with them.

[67]

VII

THE NORTHS went out to dinner. They went to Mario's, which is nearest of the places they find permissible and which has other advantages, not the least of them that it is open on Sunday evening. "Mr. and Mrs. North," Mario said, when they had gone down three steps from the sidewalk into the big, dimly lit room with red tablecloths. "Very cold, very dry, with lemon peel."

"Sometimes," Pam said, as they followed Mario to a corner table, "I feel as if I ought to be worried by that sort of greeting. Are we getting in a rut, do you think?"

"Do we want to run the risk of olives?" Jerry said, and spoke rhetorically. Whereupon, as rhetorically, Pamela North shivered.

They had a corner table; presently they had the cold and dry ones, with lemon peel. Sipping, looking, Pam said, "Do you see what I see?"

"Obviously," Jerry said, "not. Since you're looking one way and I the other."

"Look in the mirror," Pam said, with forbearance, and Jerry looked into the mirror behind his wife. He said, "I suppose so. What, in particular?" But then, before Pam answered, bothered to answer, he said, "Oh."

"Of course," Pam said, "since it was nearest for us, it was nearest for them, too. And why should they go off and eat separately— He's talking a blue streak, isn't he?"

Doug Mears, facing the girl with dark red hair at a table for two in the most distant corner of the dim room, did appear to be talking a blue streak. He seemed to be talking earnestly; he leaned forward

[68]

over the table to talk. They could see only the back of Hilda La-tham's head. She was, also, leaning a little forward, apparently to listen. Once she shook her head; a little later she nodded her head.

"Attentive," Pam said. "The story of his life, do you suppose? Or —of theirs?"

Jerry North abandoned the mirror in favor of his wife. He said, "Huh?"

"I thought so when he first came in," Pam said. "Then I wasn't sure. But of course you don't get mad at somebody you don't like."

Jerry thought of saying "Huh?" again, but decided against it. He knew what Pam meant. He guessed. This is a condition with which he is familiar.

"If he was jealous of Mr. Blanchard," Pam said, "it would be a very different dish of tea, wouldn't it? Or possibly of arsenic. Poor young man in love with a rich girl. Proud, of course. Wouldn't dream of living on his wife's money."

"The more fool he," Jerry said. "You think if you'd had money, I'd have had qualms?"

"I think," Pam said, "you'd have brought the subject up weeks before you did." She considered. "Except then we hadn't met then, had we? I mean, when I say weeks—"

"I know," Jerry said. "Go on with the synopsis, Pam. Poor but reasonably honest young tennis player—"

"Loses a match which would have got him a professional offer," Pam said. "Meanwhile, back on the farm."

"Huh?"

"The corn grows," Pam said. "All the same—it does, you know. He would have had enough money to propose. But—while he waits, Mr. Blanchard is making hay. On the same farm."

"To roll in," Jerry said, gravely.

"What a mind," Pam said. "So the wounded tennis player—why do I say 'wounded'?"

"Somebody," Jerry said, "wrote a book about one. With a title like that, as I recall. Years ago. So Mears?"

"Decides that the foot-fault calls were part of a scheme to keep him from getting a good contract, and so from marrying the girl, so that Blanchard can marry her instead. So, naturally, he kills Blanchard."

"Most natural," Jerry said. "Shall I order another rut?"

Pam thought not. She thought spaghetti, in a small dose, to be followed by scallopini. Mario, reflected in the mirror, held up two fingers and raised eyebrows. Jerry shook his head and Mario's mobile features reflected shocked surprise. But he came and Jerry ordered.

"Only," Pam said, "I wonder if she is, really? Because you'll have to admit it's a long way from anywhere."

Jerry blinked rapidly. He said he guessed he was a little slow on the uptake, but—?

"Rich," Pam said. "The apartment. Do you want me to spell it out?"

"Please," Jerry said. "I'm sorry, but please."

"The Blanchard apartment," Pam said, and spoke slowly, to a backward child. "The Blanchard apartment is what is called to hell and gone. From any place a girl like Hilda would want to go." She paused. "Except possibly Columbia University," she said. "We'll leave that out. All right?"

"Entirely. Leave it out."

"She'd come in town," Pam said, "to shop. Or go to the theater. She wouldn't get above—oh, say Fifty-seventh. But she does go way up on Riverside Drive to spend the night. Why not a hotel? The Pierre? The St. Regis? Come to that, the Waldorf? Or the Barclay? The Barclay's nice."

"Very," Jerry said. But now there was, in his voice, a note of consideration.

"Precisely," Pam said. "The kind of hotel she'd want to stay at would cost money. If daddy's got it in piles, it's one thing. If he hasn't, it's another. Riverside Drive. Free night's lodging, except for taxi fares. And there are buses."

"You've heard," Jerry said. "But—it is a point, Pam. Meanwhile, back on the farm—"

"The corn's as high as," Pam said. "Go on."

"The farm in Southampton," Jerry said. "Genteel poverty in a mansion. Beautiful daughter into the breach. Marry an older, but rich, man and restore the family fortunes. Lips a little stiff, of course. Particularly the upper. Smile a little forced. Indicating broken heart. Duty before love. I must put you out of my life forever. It is the only way."

"The things you must read," Pam North said.

"In line of duty," Jerry said. "And, don't think I don't, my dear. Oh, change a word here and there. Stream the consciousness a little. All the same—"

"He's holding hands, now," Pam said. "The left, I think."

"Eaves-peeper," Jerry said. And looked into the mirror. "The right, I think," he said.

"Mirror image," Pam said. "The left. And she's nodding her head." She paused for a moment and said, "Oh," in a disappointed voice. "They're going," Pam said. "And we haven't even started to eat."

***

Robert Sandys was a tall, thin man with heavy iron-gray hair; he was apparently in his early sixties. He wore a suit of so dark a gray that it was almost black; he wore a white shirt with a starched collar and a black knitted tie. He and his wife, he told Captain William Weigand, had been driving in the country. His wife, who was rather short and rather plump, who had one of the friendliest pink faces Bill Weigand could remember having seen, wore a black

[71]

silk dress, with white at the throat. The white, Bill guessed, made it a costume suitable for a drive into the country.

Her pink face crinkled when she heard; she cried and dabbed her eyes with a tiny white handkerchief and said, "I'm sorry, sir. I just can't help it. He was so—" She cried harder, then, and said, "Excuse me, sir. Please excuse me," and went from the apartment foyer down the corridor to her quarters.

Sandys had a long face. When he heard, his face seemed to grow older.

"We have been with Mr. Blanchard for a very long time," he said. "You must forgive my wife, captain. She was attached to Mr. Blanchard."

There was a kind of rustiness in the man's low voice; it was as if something had rusted in his throat.

They had had the weekend off, been given the weekend off. Mr. Blanchard had, very generously, allowed them the use of one of the cars. They had left Saturday morning and driven up into New Hampshire and through the mountains, and stayed overnight in Burlington, Vermont. They had returned at a little after six, although Mr. Blanchard had said that Monday would be quite soon enough. They had not wanted to inconvenience him, in the event he might have changed his plans.

"If we had been here," Robert Sandys said, and his voice was, momentarily, more than rusty.

He could not conceive that Mr. Blanchard could have had any enemies. Surely, he thought, the assailant must have been somebody who had broken in—broken in to steal. If he had been there— He and Mr. Blanchard together—

Bill suggested that Mr. Sandys sit down. "Thank you, sir," Mr. Sandys said, and continued to stand—to stand stiffly, as if at attention.

There was nothing, Bill told him, to indicate forcible entry. It seemed probable that Mr. Blanchard had let his murderer in. Or, of course, that the murderer had had a key. As to keys?

Each of the Sandyses had a key to the apartment. Mr. Blanchard of course had one.

"And Miss Latham?"

"Miss Hilda had her own key, captain. She has been notified?"

She knew. Which brought up a point—who else should be notified? Relatives?

"Mr. Blanchard had no living relatives," Sandys said. "To my knowledge, at least."

He had had the "usual" number of friends. He had entertained friends at dinner, sometimes once a week, sometimes less often. Most frequently, he had three men in to dinner, and afterward played bridge. He was a member of several clubs, including a bridge club. He was, Sandys understood, a bridge player of tournament caliber.

Women friends?

The wives of his male friends, certainly. Others? "I am afraid I am not informed as to that, captain." Miss Latham, obviously?

"Miss Hilda," Sandys said, "is the daughter of one of his oldest friends. Mr. Graham Latham."

He said this, Bill thought, with a kind of finality. Which was interesting. Or, which might be. He might, Bill thought, get further with Mrs. Sandys. But not at the moment.

It would be necessary to go through any papers Mr. Blanchard might have in the apartment. Or at his office?

"Mr. Blanchard did not maintain an office, captain. He was not in active practice as a lawyer."

Then—there were certain locked drawers. A safe. It would be necessary for the police to examine the contents of these. It would be preferable if somebody with the authority could authorize the unlocking of drawers, of safe. If necessary, of course, they could be opened without authority. If necessary, forced open.

"I can show you the keys, captain," Sandys said. "And, if that would be proper, open the safe. Mr. Blanchard—entrusted me with the combination."

"Under the circumstances," Bill said, and was faintly surprised at the formality of his own phrasing, "I think it would be entirely proper, Mr. Sandys."

The safe was precisely where one would have expected it to be —in the library, behind a picture. It was the first place the police had looked; it would have been the first place anybody would have looked. Sandys opened the safe. It had not, apparently, been rifled. At any rate, it still contained a considerable amount of cash. And, what appeared to be a will. And a key to a safe-deposit box.

In lieu of anyone else, Bill Weigand gave a receipt to Robert Sandys. He said, "You'd better go and see to that wife of yours, Mr. Sandys."

"Thank you, sir," Sandys said. "We will both be available if we can be of any service."

He went.

"This fellow Ackerman is getting pretty hot under the collar," Sergeant Mullins said, coming in from the room in which Mr. Ackerman was stored. "Says this is a hell of a note."

"Did he, really, sergeant?"

"O.K.," Mullins said. "High-handed procedure. I was just keeping it simple."

"Right," Bill said. "Get him, sergeant."

Mullins got Floyd Ackerman. He was a very thin man in a suit almost as dark as that of Sandys; he was white-faced. His head was oddly shaped and, obscurely, reminded Bill of something. Of course —of a mansard roof. He wore large and heavily rimmed eyeglasses, with very thick lenses. His eyes were strangely magnified behind the lenses. Mr. Ackerman held out one white hand and pointed it at Bill Weigand, and the hand shook.

"This is outrageous," he said. He had a high-pitched voice. "Most high-handed."

Bill was sorry. He regretted that Mr. Ackerman had had to wait. There were many things to be done.

"One hour and twelve minutes," Ackerman said, shrilly, and shook with rage. It was odd, Bill thought, that he remained so pale. "Do you think *my* time has no value? That *I* have nothing better to do? Illegal detention. I shall carry this to—" He paused, and blinked behind the thick lenses. "The highest quarters," he said. "It will be—" He paused again. "A test case." He shook the extended hand at Bill Weigand.

"Right," Bill said. "By all means, if you like. Meanwhile—you came here to see Mr. Blanchard? Not knowing he was dead?"

"Certainly," Ackerman said, in his high voice. "Obviously, I should think—"

"Why? The detective who let you in seemed to feel that you were —indignant. Said, 'Where's this man Blanchard?' in what seemed to him a rather excited way."

"What do I care what it seemed like to a—a flatfoot?" He used the outmoded term of opprobrium as if new-minted, then and there, by himself.

"Right," Bill said. "What do you care? Were you—call it indignant? Want to have something out with Mr. Blanchard?"

"Certainly," Ackerman said. "I—*scat! Scat, I say!*"

Bill was startled; realized almost at once that Ackerman's already starey eyes were fixed on something beyond him; apparently at something on the floor. Bill turned.

A black cat, rather oddly shaped, had come out from under something. Perhaps Ackerman's voice had disturbed a quiet nap. The cat stretched. The cat, even when not stretching, had an amazingly high rear end. He also had no tail whatever. With stretching finished, he sat and looked with rather detached interest at the two men who had disturbed his rest.

"Get it out of here!" Ackerman said, and his voice went higher still. "*Scat, you!*"

It did not appear that the Manx cat had had the meaning of the word "scat" explained to him. He looked up at Ackerman and closed his eyes, a little wearily.

And Floyd Ackerman moved forward and kicked at the cat.

He did not, of course, kick the cat. The Manx took care of that. The Manx also hissed, briefly and with contempt.

"I'd leave him alone," Bill Weigand said, and spoke sharply.

"I'll do—" Ackerman began, and Bill Weigand said, "You'll not kick cats around," and went to the door and opened it. The Manx walked through the door with such dignity as the built-in gait of a Manx cat permits. Outside he turned and hissed again, and then he went.

"If I want to kick cats—" Ackerman began, but Bill said, "Skip it. You did want to have something out with Mr. Blanchard? Came here this afternoon—evening—with that in mind?"

"To tell him," Ackerman said, "to retract or be sued. To let him understand that I would not take such—aspersions—lying down. To make it clear that—"

"Wait," Bill said and, a little unexpectedly, Ackerman waited. "You're talking about Mr. Blanchard's letter? In this morning's *Times*?"

"Certainly. Flagrantly libelous. A flat accusation that I am—*immoral*. Also, I'll sue the *Times* for printing it. Not for myself. Certainly not for myself. For The Cause." The capitalization was Ackerman's, by intonation.

Jerry had told Bill Weigand that Ackerman was a fanatic. "A lit-

[76]

tle hipped," Jerry had said. It occurred to Bill that Jerry had under-stated.

"I've read the letter," Bill said. "As I recall it, Mr. Blanchard found an attitude immoral. Not you. Or your committee."

"Crying fire *in a crowded theater*," Ackerman said, and shook. His eyes seemed abnormally large behind the glasses. His pale hair lay flat on what Bill still found it hard not to think of as his mansard roof. Bill would have expected it to bristle. "These sadistic torturers of helpless creatures!"

From a man who had just tried, however ineptly, to kick a cat, the indignation Ackerman displayed seemed to come oddly. Bill Weigand avoids side issues, however tempting, when possible. He could not quite avoid this one.

"You tried to kick the cat," Bill said, mildly.

"What," Ackerman said, "has that got to do with it? It's a matter of principle. It is not necessary to like cats."

"Right," Bill said. "Of course not."

It occurred to him that it was perhaps more necessary, from where Ackerman stood, to dislike people. Especially, of course, scientists. "Skip it," Bill told himself.

"I take it," Bill said, "that you had just read Mr. Blanchard's letter? Before you came here to—demand a retraction? An apology?"

"Certainly not," Ackerman said. "I never sleep later than six." He spoke with pride. "Never," he said, clinching it home.

The hiatus was obvious. Bill stepped across it.

"So," he said, "you read the letter this morning. Early, apparently. And—waited all day before coming to take it up with Mr. Blan-chard?"

He put scepticism into the question. Not that there was any rea-son Ackerman shouldn't have waited—no reason but Ackerman him-self, a man atremble with zeal; a man, Bill thought, not likely to come slowly to a boil, but to boil at once.

[77]

"When I first—" Ackerman said, and bit it off. The magnifying lenses hid whatever expression might then have come into Ackerman's light blue eyes.

"Right," Bill said. "When you first came here—what, Mr. Ackerman?"

"Nobody answered the bell," Ackerman said. "All right—I did try earlier. About—oh, half past nine."

"At," Bill said, "somewhere around the time he was killed."

He didn't ask. He said. Then he asked.

"How did you know that, Mr. Ackerman? If you didn't know he was dead?"

Floyd Ackerman said he didn't know what Weigand meant.

"Come now," Weigand said. "You're obviously an intelligent man, Mr. Ackerman. Admitting you'd been here earlier was a slip of the tongue. So, you had been trying to keep that secret. If you didn't know you were here about the time he was killed, why keep it secret?"

"You're trying to trick me. I might have—"

"No. Why?"

"I didn't know the time," Ackerman said. "When I came here I had no idea anything had happened to him. It was merely that I saw no reason to—to—"

"Put ideas in our heads?"

He could call it that. Ideas which would serve no purpose; would merely obscure the truth. His tone capitalized "The Truth." He had a very capitalizing style, Bill decided.

"You rang the bell," Bill said. "At about nine thirty. Nobody answered. You didn't see anybody. Hear anything from inside the apartment. You went away and came back—hours later. That's what you say?"

"Certainly. There was a meeting this afternoon. Of the committee. To consider an answer to—to this libelous attack on Our Work.

[78]

It was agreed that I should seek a retraction. I thought it best to—confront Blanchard. In Person."

"Which you had already tried to do. Without consulting the committee."

"I," Ackerman said simply, "am the chairman. Also, if you must know, I raise the money."

Bill had felt under no compulsion to know that. He did not in the least mind knowing it.

Ackerman had heard nothing inside the apartment, except the ringing, distant, of the doorbell. He had seen no one.

"When you went into the lobby downstairs," Weigand said. "This morning, I mean. You knew which elevator to take?"

"No. I took the first one I saw. Are there others?"

"One. You had a fifty-fifty chance. Mr. Ackerman, was the elevator waiting? At the lobby floor?"

And then, Bill thought, Ackerman hesitated. It was as if, once more, he had a fifty-fifty chance. Then he said, "No. It came down when I pushed the button."

"Empty?"

Ackerman did not hesitate this time. He spoke, Bill thought, almost too quickly when he said, "Of course it was empty. I've already said—"

"I know," Bill Weigand said. "Right. I won't take up any more of your time just now."

Ackerman, Bill thought, looked a little surprised.

"Give your address to one of the men outside," Bill said. "We may want to talk to you again."

Ackerman was still shaking when he went out. He had lied about the elevator, Bill thought. Protecting someone else? It occurred to Bill that Ackerman might well try to protect anyone who had killed John Blanchard. Particularly, of course, a white-faced man named Floyd Ackerman.

[79]

VIII

THE NORTHS walked back from Mario's. On the way, they mooted a point—should they tell Bill Weigand that Doug Mears and Hilda Latham had had dinner together, had seemed more friendly than they had appeared to be earlier, had seemed to have important things to talk about? (Or, he to talk about, she to listen to.) Because, Pam said, it would be a case of peep and tell, but on the other hand.

She, Jerry said as they turned into their block, put it very neatly.

"If they were only talking about themselves," Pam said, clarifying, "no, of course. But if he was explaining that it was perfectly all right for him to have killed Blanchard—what's he doing down here?"

She pointed, not at a man. She pointed at a pale yellow Cadillac, parked at the curb. It was parked within inches of a fire hydrant. Its license plate bore, along with a number, the letters DVS.

"Attending a cat," Jerry said.

They turned into their apartment house. Dr. Oscar Gebhardt, cat specialist, sat on a stone bench. He did, Pam thought, brighten up the lobby, dressed as he was for his Sunday rounds. (He had explained that several times: When a man works twelve hours a day, seven days a week, it becomes difficult to tell days apart. If one cannot rest on the Sabbath, one can at least relax in costume.) Gebhardt got up from the bench and came toward the Norths, his eyebrows bristling. He said he had been about ready to give them up.

"Gebby," Jerry North said, "do you know you're parked in front of a fire plug?"

"Obviously," Gebhardt said. "Only place I could find."

Which, clearly, settled that. What Oscar Gebhardt paid in traffic fines would have kept him in taxicabs for life, a fact he cheerfully admitted. But he preferred to drive the Cadillac. For one thing, his calls frequently took him far from the city. For another, he liked to drive Cadillacs.

"Happened to be down here," Gebhardt said, in the elevator going up. "Thought I'd say hello."

"Hello, Gebby," Pam said. "Do you know where I can get a Siamese that isn't pointed?"

"Hard thing to do," Gebhardt said, as Jerry let them into the apartment. "Damn near all of them are pointed. Damn fool cat people."

"I'll make coffee," Pam said.

"Can't stay long," Oscar Gebhardt said, sitting down and putting his black bag on the floor beside him. "Got a very bad vitamin deficiency in Sutton Place. Keep feeding him crab meat. The things people feed cats!"

Pam went into the kitchen. Oscar Gebhardt looked around the room. "Strange not to see her here," he said. "Spunky little thing, wasn't she?"

"Yes," Jerry said, and spoke in a low tone and looked toward the open kitchen door.

"All right," Gebhardt said. "I'll keep my mouth shut. She still cry?"

"Not as much," Jerry said, and then Pam came back, and said it wouldn't be a minute. She looked at Gebhardt's hard, wonderfully deft, hands. There was a new bandage now, this one on the left index finger. Cats are more deft than the deftest hands.

"Intestinal stoppage," Gebhardt said. "Came from eating mouse bones. And hide, of course. Damn fool owner was afraid to get a good grip. Afraid she'd break. Look—I take it you two know these policemen?"

"Yes," Pam said. "For a long time, Gebby."

"The big one," Gebhardt said, "is a pain in the neck. You tell him the truth and where does it get you?"

[81]

"Mullins," Jerry said. "Sergeant Mullins. It got him scratched."

"Bitten," Gebhardt said.

"You could have had one of us hold her," Pam said. "We know how. Poor Mullins."

"I weep for him," Gebhardt said, with sudden gaiety. He sobered. "Look," he said, "are they going to get the idea I killed John? Make a hell of a lot of trouble about it? Because, I haven't got time to waste on that sort of thing."

Oscar Gebhardt seemed very serious about it. He seemed, further, to be rather concerned about it.

"Mullins had to find out," Pam said. "Nobody'll think you had anything to do with it. Why should they?"

"No reason," Gebhardt said. "Anyway—no, no reason."

Pam said, "It's boiling by now," and went, and, within minutes, returned with coffee on a tray.

"All right, Gebby," Jerry North said, when the coffee had been served. "Let's have it."

Gebhardt looked astonished—or, they both thought, tried to look astonished. He said there was nothing for anybody to have. He said the coffee was very fine coffee.

"You want what?" Jerry said. "Intercession? For us to tell Bill Weigand you're not the kind of man who goes around killing people? Particularly clients. We'll be glad to, Gebby. But listen—"

Gebby listened, while Gerald North said the obvious, carefully. Policemen like Weigand are impartial. They are also shrewd, also experienced. A person who says he found a man dying, a person who has a key to the apartment in which the man dies—obviously, he must explain himself. As obviously, Gebhardt had. Which would end it.

"In a word," Pam said, "you're making a mountain, Gebby."

Which, she thought, isn't at all like you, Gebby.

Gebhardt listened, he nodded his head. He sipped coffee. He

[82]

said he probably was making a mountain. Then he said, "Only—"

They looked at him.

"All right," he said, "John left me somewhere around two hundred thousand dollars, I imagine. When they find out about it—well. There you are."

"My," Pam said. "What a lot of money."

"To," Gebhardt said, "start a research hospital—center—with. But whether his will makes that clear—" He shrugged, wide shoulders under the reddish tweed jacket. "Of course," he said, and brightened, "could be he changed his mind. Couple of years ago he told me about it." They waited. "It was this way," Gebhardt said.

A couple of years ago, with a patient attended to, Blanchard and Dr. Gebhardt, over coffee, had discussed cats—cats in general. And, to sympathetic ears, Oscar Gebhardt had expanded on an idea he had had long in mind, and expected never to do anything about— an idea that, some time, somebody should do something about.

Veterinary medicine lacked research facilities. Gebhardt did not argue that the need for such facilities had a high order of precedence. Other things should, obviously, come first. "But not," he said now, with some bitterness, "shooting skyrockets at the moon." Also, concentrated research on the diseases of animals—and particularly of small animals—would almost inevitably carry the possibility of greater usefulness. "Incidentally," Gebhardt said, "where do people think Pasteur started? Anthrax. That's where. Bunch of sheep. Damn silly things, sheep."

Gebhardt did not contend that much valuable work was not being done. At, for example, Cornell. But not enough. With enough money—

"Well," he said, "I got steamed up about it. Told John what I'd like to do would be to start a hospital which would be, mainly, a research center and really find out a few things. Not that I don't know more than most. But none of us knows enough."

[83]

Gebhardt supposed that, unconsciously, he had been making a pitch. But it had been unconscious, he insisted, and the Norths believed. He had ridden a hobby, with no destination in mind.

He had, he said—and the Norths believed—been vastly surprised when, a few months later (while he was treating another Blanchard cat) John Blanchard had said, casually, "By the way, Gebby. About that research hospital of yours. I'm leaving you some money for it. Enough to get it started, anyway. What you said would get it started."

Gebhardt had said that to build, equip, get going, something like two hundred thousand dollars would be necessary. If they were really to do a job.

"I guess my mouth fell open," he said, talking now to the Norths. "Anyway, he said, 'Only, Gebby, I never felt better in my life, so don't get your hopes up.' Since he was only a couple of years older than I am, and in, from the looks of him, a hell of a lot better condition, I didn't get them up." He paused. "That sounds wrong," he said. "John—I liked John." He paused and finished his coffee. He said, well, there they had it.

"This bequest," Jerry said. "Would it be to—some sort of a foundation? Or, for a specified purpose? Or—just to you, Gebby?"

"To me, I gathered," Gebhardt said. "No strings. John wouldn't have tied strings to it, I imagine. I don't actually know. It would make a difference, wouldn't it? In the way it looked?"

"It might," Jerry said. "But I don't think you've got anything to worry about, really. Bill Weigand's not a man to jump at things. And, he'll listen to things. I wouldn't worry."

"This man you call Mullins," Gebhardt said, with doubt.

Weigand, they told him, was the man who would decide, the man to be considered. Not that Mullins wouldn't listen, too. Not that Mullins pushed people around.

Gebhardt seemed to accept that statement with some scepticism.

He said, but with doubt, that after all, they knew Mullins and he didn't. His eyebrows, Pam thought, didn't bristle quite so resolutely. She offered, he took, another cup of coffee. She changed the subject. Did he know anything about a Madeline Somers? Who, it appeared, ran a cat store?

He did. He knew most people who associated themselves with cats.

As pet shops went, that of Miss Somers was pretty good. He didn't argue that it was a place to go for a prize cat. He didn't argue that there were not some cats on sale at Miss Somers's "store" who were culls from established catteries. But—the cats Miss Somers had for sale were healthy cats. He knew the "vet"—he paused, corrected himself, said "veterinarian"—who checked on them. They would be inoculated. And it might, at that, be a place to find a Siamese who wasn't pointed.

"Because," he said, "you don't win prizes with them now unless they are, and more's the pity. So a cattery might let a cat with a cat's face go cheap. Not, Mrs. North, that your Miss Somers is going to."

There was only one thing he knew against Miss Madeline Somers. She was one of some damn fool collection of crackpots who called themselves "The Committee Against Cruelty." They had tried to get Dr. Oscar Gebhardt to lend his support, and he had told them where to jump.

"Crackpots," he repeated. "And that man Ackerman—ought to be locked up. Happen to read that advertisement?"

They had.

"John wrote a letter taking their hides off," Gebhardt said. "Showed it to me a couple of days ago. Don't know whether he sent it to anybody."

He had, they told him. He had sent it to the *Times*. Which had printed it.

"Don't have time for the papers," Gebhardt said. "Make this nut Ackerman sore as hell, I'd think. No telling what a crackpot—" He stopped, abruptly. He looked from Pam to Jerry and back to Pam again. He told them he'd be damned.

***

Sergeant Mullins did not precisely say he had told anybody so. For one thing, he admitted to himself that he had not. Which was not to say he had not had his thoughts. Red coat and green pants, and said he was a doctor.

"Helluva lot of money to leave to a cat doctor," Mullins did say. "Must have been pretty damn fond of cats, this Blanchard."

There was only one answer to be made to this, and Bill Weigand made it—"Right." It was a hell of a lot of money to leave to anybody. Two hundred thousand dollars is a hell of a lot of money. "To my friend, Oscar Gebhardt, to be used at his discretion for purposes we have discussed, the sum of two hundred thousand dollars."

"Build an old cats' home, you think?" Mullins suggested.

Bill smiled mildly, and said he didn't think anything one way or the other, having no material for thought. Except, again, that it was a lot of money to leave to anybody.

It was evident that John Blanchard had had a lot of money—or had thought he had. Or had had at the time, some eighteen months before, when he had made his last will and testament, of which the document they had found in the safe was a copy. (The will had been drawn up by Cameron, Notson and Fleigel, which, it was to be assumed, had retained the original. Cameron, Notson and Fleigel would be consulted.)

Substantial as it was, the bequest to Dr. Oscar Gebhardt was not the largest provided. The largest was to Hilda Latham, of Southampton, Long Island, and was in the amount of half a million dollars. "Phew!" Mullins said, hitting the nail on the head. "Why?"

[86]

Nothing in the will answered that question, and it puzzled Bill Weigand. The daughter of an old friend—yes. A young woman toward whom Blanchard—"Uncle John" of other days—might have felt as toward a favorite niece. But still—

He had gathered, although from no specific facts, that the Lathams were in no need of money. He checked his memory, seeking the grounds for this assumption. Except that Hilda, after saying that her father was Graham Latham, had hesitated momentarily, as if identification of the name was to be expected—as if the name were almost as likely to be identified as, say, Rockefeller. Graham Latham, Southampton, membership in the West Side Tennis Club —there were implications of the luxurious. Of course, even people with a great deal of money do not, presumably, mind being given more. And do, Bill thought, seem uncommonly likely to be given more. But still—

"You know," Mullins said, "it's kind of a funny thing she'd come all the way up here to save a hotel bill. Ain't it? Won't need to now, will she?"

Bill looked at Mullins thoughtfully. He was not surprised; he does not underestimate Sergeant Mullins. He was, admittedly, a little chagrined at having missed a point. However—

Robert and Helen Sandys (or the survivor), if in Blanchard's employment at the time of his death, were to receive fifty thousand dollars and the apartment, which Blanchard owned, and there were no strings to this, either—no requirement that they provide for whatever cats were also surviving (and in Blanchard's employment) at the time of his death. From the little he had seen of the Sandyses, Bill supposed that no such stipulation was necessary, and that Blanchard had known it.

There was a clause directing the executors of the estate to set aside a sufficient sum from the residue to provide an annual scholarship of two thousand dollars to be given to "the boy, not over seventeen, who shall, in the opinion of the selection committee of the United States Lawn Tennis Association, be, in any year, the most promising junior player of United States citizenship, providing that he is financially unable to start, or to continue in, study at the college or university of his choice."

The remainder of the estate—"Remainder?" Mullins said, in a tone of some incredulity—was to be divided evenly among the Greenwich Village Humane Society, the Authors' League Fund and the ASPCA.

They were sitting at a desk in Blanchard's office, Mullins at the end of the desk. A long-haired red cat leaped (and where had he been?) onto the other end of the desk, reached out a paw, and delicately patted the will of his late master.

"My God," Sergeant Mullins said. "All over the place, ain't they, loot?" He looked at the red, who looked at him with considerable interest. "All kinds, too," Mullins said. "You'd think—"

What you would think did not immediately become apparent. They were interrupted. A long thin man with a long sad face stood in the open doorway. "Dope from downtown," he said, unhappily. He held papers out to Weigand. "Interesting, sort of," he said. The fact seemed to depress him. "Gives an angle," Nathan Shapiro said. "Only, pretty confusing. To me." He went mournfully out. The cat went with him.

Bill looked. He said, "Well, well," and handed the laboratory reports to Mullins. Mullins said he'd be damned. He did, Bill thought, seem a little disappointed.

On a corner of the base of one of the cat-scratching posts, the lab men had found two human hairs. They had also found hairs of several cats—a black cat, a brownish cat, a reddish cat. They had found several paw marks—hind-paw marks—on the surface of the base. The red cat, from the length of the hair, apparently was a Persian.

The human hairs conformed to specimens provided by the mortuary, from the head of the late John Blanchard. There were no visible vestiges of blood on any corner of any of the three posts submitted. Chemical analysis had not been completed.

"Wouldn't have to be," Mullins said. "Just caved in. Didn't bleed much."

There were no fingerprints on any of the bases. The carpet covering of the posts would not, of course, take prints.

Two tennis rackets had been submitted, both in covers and presses. The wood of one of the presses was too rough to take prints; the wood of the other—this one rectangular; the other a truncated triangle—was smooth enough to take prints. The prints, all apparently made some time ago, were those of the deceased (these the most numerous) and of another man. The latter were fragmentary, inadequate for identification. "Probably Sandys's," Bill said.

Both rackets had leather grips. On one of them were the prints, again not recent, of the deceased. On the other were also prints left by John Blanchard and, overlying them, much more recent prints which coincided with prints taken from a glass submitted at the direction of Captain William Weigand, but not identified by him. These prints were in such position on the racket handle as to indicate that the unknown person, almost certainly male, had held the racket, recently, as he might in play, employing the standard Eastern grip.

They looked at each other.

"For once," Mullins said, "it ain't going to be screwy. Even if the Norths are in it." But then a shadow passed over his ruddy face. "I hope," Mullins said. "Only—you suppose it's *too* easy, loot? Because, after all, they are."

That was at a little after nine in the evening. Doug Mears did not show up at the Forest Hills Inn, where he was staying, until a little after eleven thirty. He was awaited; he was taken to Manhattan, to the offices of the Homicide Squad in West Twentieth Street.

IX

IT WAS PAM who made up their minds for them. She said it was simple, really. She said, "Listen, dear," and Jerry listened.

"If it was just boy meets girl over spaghetti," she said, "then there's no reason why we shouldn't, because what difference would it make? They've a perfect right, so far as we know. Not as if either of them was married to somebody else. Unless, of course, one of them is. Anyway—if it's only that, there's no harm in our telling Bill. But if it isn't only that, and has something to do with this, there'd be harm in our not telling, or might be, and anyway Bill ought to decide and how can he if we don't?"

She paused; looked at Jerry expectantly.

"It was a little simpler before you explained it," Jerry said. "But —I suppose you're right. Makes me feel a little like a divorce snooper."

Pam said she didn't see why he complicated things by bringing divorce into it. She said nobody had said anything about a divorce. She pointed out that people have to be married before they can be divorced, and that if he was going to be sensitive about it she'd just as soon call. After all, she was the one who had seen them first, so the responsibility was hers.

It was eleven forty-five then, and Pam telephoned first to Bill's office, with a call to his apartment in reserve. The second call proved unnecessary.

Bill said, "Weigand," and Pam said, "Pam," which made a nice start. She told him then, and now was succinct as she can be when the mood is on her, about the presence together at Mario's of Doug

Mears and Hilda Latham and of the outer semblances—the hand held, the intentness in the man's face—of some tie between the two which they had not revealed earlier when they met at the Norths' apartment.

It did not, Pam pointed out, have to mean anything. They had merely thought he ought to know, since the decision as to what things meant was his.

"Right," Bill said. He hesitated, feeling that the presence of Deputy Chief Inspector Artemus O'Malley hovered over him. (A very red-faced presence; Inspector O'Malley has strong feeling about the Norths; it amounts to Northophobia.) "As a matter of fact," Bill said, "Mears has just been brought in to—explain a thing or two."

"Bill!"

"Not now," Bill said. "In time, Pamela. As always. Good night, Pamela."

***

Bill Weigand, having hung up, considered the telephone. It fitted in—was a piece in a picture which was forming. A young man and a young woman with more to talk about than they had seemed to have; a bequest which was certainly what people called "substantial"; fingerprints where no fingerprints should—

"All right," Bill said, to Mullins. "Have him brought in. And a stenographer."

"Formal like?"

"Right," Bill said. "I think so, sergeant."

They brought Doug Mears in. He moved, for all his length, in spite of what was almost angularity in his long body, with lithe grace. His face was set, angry. He said, "Now what?" in a hard voice and stood in front of Bill Weigand's desk.

"Sit down, Mr. Mears," Bill said, and Mears didn't, and Bill seemed not to notice this. "There are a few more questions we'd like to ask you. In connection with Mr. Blanchard's death."

"I don't," Mears said, "know a damn thing more than I've told you."

"Then," Bill said, "we'll just go over that again. It may take some little time. You may as well sit down."

This time Mears sat down. He leaned forward. There was truculence in the shape of his body.

"Am I charged with anything?" he said. "Let's get that straight."

"No. You're not charged with anything. At the moment."

"Suppose I don't want to answer questions? You try to beat answers out of me?"

Bill sighed. He made the sigh audible.

"No," he said. "We don't beat anything out of you. You don't have to say anything, answer anything. We can charge you—say as a material witness. That's a very handy charge. You can get a lawyer to represent you when you're arraigned tomorrow before a magistrate. Then you'll find out why you were asked to come here."

"*Asked*," Mears said, with bitterness.

"Very well," Bill said. "Why you were brought here. You're wasting everybody's time, Mr. Mears." Mears glared at him. "Right," Bill said. "Sergeant, take Mr. Mears down to the desk. Book him as a material witness in the homicidal death of John Blanchard. Let him make the telephone call he's entitled to make. Then—"

"O.K.," Mears said. "I've got nothing to tell you. But, O.K. Shoot."

"Mr. Mears," Bill said, "you say that when you went to Mr. Blanchard's apartment this afternoon—went to get a drink he'd offered you—that that was the first time you'd been there today?"

"You're damned right I do."

"When you went there you found the police in charge," Bill said. "You were asked to go downtown to the apartment of Mr. and Mrs. North. You—"

"Asked hell," Mears said.

Bill sighed again; again made the patient sigh audible.

"You weren't in the Blanchard apartment alone, were you?" Bill said. "Let wander around it alone?"

"I didn't get beyond the foyer. You ought to know that."

"Oh," Bill said. "I do, Mr. Mears. You had no chance, then, to go to a hall closet off the foyer and get anything out of it. Touch anything. Right?"

Mears didn't bother to answer, which was enough answer.

"Then," Bill said, "suppose you tell me how your fingerprints got on the handle grip of a tennis racket Mr. Blanchard kept in the hall closet? Got there very recently. Almost certainly in the last twenty-four hours."

"What the—"

"Wait. A racket in a press. Which may have been used as the weapon by whoever killed Mr. Blanchard."

"You're trying to pull something. Running a bluff."

The words were firm enough. They had come after a considerable pause. They had come after a change in the expression on Mears's young face. You can't take a change of expression into court. However—

"No," Bill said. "They were there, Mears. Right where they would be if you had held the racket to—hit a tennis ball. Or—to hit something else. Well?"

Mears said nothing. He continued to lean forward. But the truculence had gone.

"When did they get there? When you used the racket as a club? To kill Blanchard?"

There was another longish pause.

"I didn't kill Blanchard," Mears said then, and spaced the words out slowly. He paused again. "O.K.," he said, "I've been holding out. Because it didn't mean anything and—wouldn't look good. I—I didn't think about prints on the grip. All right, I was there—"

"Wait," Bill said. "If you are going to change what you told us before, what you say now will be taken down by a stenographer. It will be written up in the form of a statement and you'll be asked to sign it. Such a statement can be introduced into evidence in court. You realize that?"

"O.K.," Mears said, and sounded very weary. "O.K. I heard you. So—I did go there in the morning. I did handle the racket. I didn't hit him with it, or hit anything with it. It was this way—"

What he said about meeting John Blanchard the previous evening at Forest Hills was true. He had apologized; he had asked whether, at some time that was convenient, Blanchard would show him what was wrong about the way he served. "They keep on changing the damn foot-fault rule," Mears said, aggrieved. Blanchard had suggested the following evening, if Mears happened then to be in town.

That morning, Mears had waked up early, and in a broody mood. He was out of the men's singles, which was what mattered. He had admitted earlier, when he first talked to Weigand, that it mattered. But—he still had a semi-finals in the mixed doubles; something that might be salvaged. "I didn't know then Nellie'd been on the—" he said, and suddenly flushed and said, perhaps to some distant Nellie, "Sorry."

If an explanation of his foot-faulting was to do him any good at Forest Hills, even the little good of getting somewhere in the mixed doubles, he would have to get it before the match. Not in the evening, after it. So, he had telephoned John Blanchard. At about eight thirty.

"Eight thirty? On a Sunday morning?"

Blanchard had a match to umpire—a semi-finals in the men's senior division. Because rain had postponed some matches earlier in the week, there had been a jam-up in schedules. The match Blanchard had agreed to umpire was set for ten in the morning. So if Blanhard wasn't up in his apartment on Riverside Drive by eight thirty, he'd damn well better be.

He had been. He had hesitated; he had said O.K., if Mears would be quick about it. With almost no traffic, Mears had been able to be quick. He had rung the doorbell of the apartment at about nine o'clock. Blanchard had been fully dressed; had warned that he didn't have much time.

"He showed me," Mears said. "You want the details? It's easier to show than to explain. That's why—"

"Never mind that now," Bill said. "So?"

"The way he saw it," Mears said, "when I went across the line I touched down with the free foot before I hit—"

"Never mind," Bill said. "I'm not a tennis player."

"Could have been," Mears said, looking at Bill Weigand across the desk. "Even now, if you—"

Bill smiled for the first time. It was not a prolonged smile. Bill shook his head. He said, "Get on with it, Mr. Mears."

Blanchard had demonstrated, using the edge of a carpet as a base line. Mears had gone through motions; he hadn't, he said now, seemed quite to get it. It was Blanchard who suggested that it might be easier if he actually swung a racket, who had said there was one in the hall closet, if he wanted to try it; had said, again, that they'd have to hurry.

Mears said he had got the racket; had not wasted time removing the press or cover; had simulated a few service swings.

Bill looked at the long young man, mentally added the length of a racket to an arm.

"Just could," Mears said. "Damned high ceilings in that old place."

There were. Bill remembered that.

Mears thought he had it. Blanchard had promised that, if he got a chance, he would watch Mears play during the afternoon. If Mears wanted to, he could drop by in the evening—around six—and learn what Blanchard had seen. Meanwhile—Blanchard, Mears told them, had looked at his watch and Mears had taken the hint and left. He had offered to drive the older man to Forest Hills, and been thanked, and told that Blanchard wanted his own car along.

Mears was not sure, but he thought he had put the racket back in the closet. He had left Blanchard in the apartment. "He was all right then." It had been, then, only about nine fifteen.

Had Mears got, in any way, an impression that Blanchard was expecting anybody else? Had another appointment?

For a moment, Bill Weigand thought, the young tennis player looked hopeful. Looked as if he saw an opening?

"No," Mears said, "I can't say I did—or come to that, didn't. He didn't say anything about one."

"Right," Bill said. "That's a very interesting explanation, Mr. Mears. Clears up that point."

"Does it?"

"Say it does," Bill said. "Now—how well do you know Miss Latham, Mr. Mears? Perhaps better than you—either of you—let on this afternoon?"

For a moment it appeared that Mears was going to get up from the chair he sat in—get up with violence. He did not. But his voice was hard again as he said, "Now, what the hell?"

Bill Weigand merely waited.

"I don't get it," Mears said, and the puzzlement in his voice was obvious—possibly too obvious. "She's a nice girl. I meet a lot of nice girls on the circuit. How well do I know her? Like I know a lot of nice girls."

"Mr. Mears," Bill said, "when you and she left the Norths this evening it seemed to me that you more or less ordered her to come with you. As if you had a right to order—a right based on—let's call it on a relationship. And you and she went to dinner together."

"What's so damn—" Mears began, and then his face flushed. "You had us followed?" he said. "What the hell gives you the right?"

"Never mind," Bill said. "You went to a place called Mario's. Your attitude there—yours and hers—was not as casual as if—say as if she were any nice girl you'd happened to come across on what you call the circuit. It appeared you had a good deal in common."

"Slipped up, didn't you?" Mears said. "No hidden mike? No lip-readers stationed at suitable places? My, my, captain?"

He overdid it. Even as he spoke, there was something in his face which suggested his own realization that he was overdoing it.

"Anyway," he said, "it's none of your damn business."

"Anything that has to do—"

"This doesn't. Blanchard was an old friend of her family. She'd known him since she was a kid. She—"

"She told me that," Bill said. "Also, that you were just one of the tennis players she knew—the tennis-playing kids, she said."

"So? Just what I—"

"Mears," Weigand said, "suppose you listen a minute. We like to do things the quick way—get facts from people who haven't anything to hide. Anything important to hide. But we can do things the slow way. And we can hold you as a material witness while we do. We can talk to people who know you and Miss Latham. People who have seen you together. People to whom you may have talked when there wasn't any reason to be cagey. Other men and women you've—oh, had dinner with, gone dancing with. We'll find people who were observant, assuming there was anything to observe. All that will slow things up. Take days instead of minutes. You and Miss Latham are merely casual acquaintances?"

"That's what I—" Mears said, and stopped.

Weigand waited again, watched the considering face of the lanky young man. It was not a poker face. It occurred to Bill Weigand that Hilda Latham had been right when she had said that, whatever his age, Mears was a "kid." Now he was an uncertain kid, carrying on a debate in his own mind, the wavering between courses reflected in his face.

"All right," Mears said. "I want to marry her. Has that anything to do with you?"

"I don't know," Bill said. "Has it, Mr. Mears? How does she feel about it?"

Mears hesitated. He said, "All right, I guess." He stopped again. "O.K.," he said, "she feels fine about it. Only—"

Weigand waited.

"Only," Mears said, "I'm a tennis bum. A pretty good one, in spite of losing to Ted Wilson. Ought to have taken him. Maybe have taken Farthing. So. I've missed it this year. Could be I'll miss it next year and the year after. Could be I'll never get it. You don't have a hell of a lot of years, unless you're a Gar Mulloy. And then —then what? Unless you've made a stake as a pro, then what?" He looked at Weigand as if he expected an answer. Bill had no answer. "My people," Doug Mears said, "haven't got any money. Just get along."

"If you feel that way—" Bill said.

"Because I like to play tennis—like it more than anything else. Because maybe one of these days—maybe next year—I'll be tops. Because—why does anybody do anything? Except clerk in a store?"

He was earnest, then. It occurred to Bill Weigand, oddly, unexpectedly, that Doug Mears was as much in earnest as a young poet might be, asked why he wrote poetry. Or a painter or— It also occurred to Bill Weigand that he was himself a policeman because he wanted to be.

"Mr. Mears," Bill said, "do you know that Miss Latham inherits a very substantial sum from Mr. Blanchard? It's—" Bill paused for a moment and considered. He saw no reason why not. "The sum is half a million dollars," he said. "Did you know that?"

[98]

Mears said "No." He said it quickly.

"Did she?"

"She's never said so."

"Right," Bill said. "So it's going to be a pleasant surprise?"

For all Mears knew. But it did not seem to Bill that, to Mears, it came as a surprise of magnitude—a surprise appropriate to the size of the inheritance, which was certainly of magnitude. Unless, of course—

"Is Miss Latham's father a rich man?"

"Now what the hell—"

"Wait," Bill said. "Let's not get off on this what-the-hell business again. You and Hilda Latham are planning to get married—thinking about it, anyway. You talk about yourselves. A lot about yourselves. About all the things that concern yourselves."

"No," Mears said. "They've got this big place, and I guess they did have money. But—now I guess not."

He looked, quickly, at the stenographer, who was making quicker movements with pencil, on notebook.

"No," Bill said. "This isn't part of the statement. You've given us an account of your actions at pertinent times. We'll ask you to sign that. Not this."

"This," Mears said, "is just fishing. In the hope you can get something on—" It seemed to reach him, then. He stood up, very tall, face red under tan. *"Damn you to hell,"* he said. He spoke loudly.

Mullins moved toward him.

Bill Weigand seemed to pay no attention to these movements.

"Mr. Mears," Weigand said, "Mr. Blanchard was an old man from where you stand. I suppose he was. He was in his late fifties. But he was a vigorous man, from all accounts. And from the appearance of his body. He might have lived a good many years. Twenty—perhaps even thirty."

Mears glared down at him.

"A half million dollars is a lot to leave to a young woman who is—" Bill hesitated. "Who is merely the daughter of an old friend. Don't you think so?"

Mears did not change position; he did not stop glaring. But the hot color under his tan lessened—lessened markedly. His lips became very tight.

"Well?" Bill said.

Mears shook his head. In denial? Or, in stupefaction that a man could be so wrong, so obtuse?

"A vigorous man," Bill said. "A man in his fifties, Mears, isn't limited to the role of—say the role of an uncle. You must know—"

"*You—*" Mears said. "*You lying—*"

Bill Weigand has been called all the usual names, and some unusual ones. All occupations have their hazards.

"Sit down, Mears," Mullins said. "Sit down and shut your mouth."

Mears turned on Mullins. Mullins was as tall as Mears, and considerably heavier. Mullins said, *"Now!"* Mears sat down. He continued to look, intently, at Bill Weigand. Finally, he said, "I suppose you've got to be like this?"

"Right," Bill said. "I've got to be like this. Well?"

"Damn it all," Mears said. "She was fond of him. Everything else aside—the kind of person she is—the— Aside from all that, she was fond of him. Had been since she was a child."

If a job makes a man, at times, a terrier, he has to learn to shake like one.

"It is possible," Bill Weigand said, "to work up considerable affection for half a million dollars. If Blanchard had lived out his life, Miss Latham might have had to wait a long time for the money, mightn't she? Conceivably, until she, too, was in her fifties. A long time for a girl whose family has a big house and not the kind of money that ought to go with it. A girl, say, who was brought up in the environment of those who do have a lot of money. A girl—"

[100]

"Damn it all," Mears said. "Let it lie, can't you?"

"No. Why should I?"

"Because," Mears said, and seemed triumphant. "Because if the money mattered that much to Hildy, all she had to do was to say, 'Yes. I'll marry you.' There wouldn't have been anything hard about that. She was fond of him. He was an all-right guy, I guess. And—he sure as hell wasn't doddering. So—"

He stopped abruptly. Bill could watch the triumph die as Mears listened to his own words.

"Mr. Mears," Bill said, "had she ever said, 'Yes, I'll marry you,' to Blanchard. Say—*before you and she met?* Was that the reason for the bequest? So that his fiancée would be taken care of if something happened to him before they were married? And then did he find out how things were between you and her and, maybe, say that under the circumstances he might decide to make a change—"

"Damn you! No!"

"You're sure? She'd never—oh, say, implied to Blanchard that she might marry him? Even if not saying, in so many words, that she would?"

"Oh, that," Mears said. "This thing about the will. I'm damned sure there was nothing about that. I'm damned sure she didn't even know he was leaving her all that money. As to what she may have said to Blanchard, before—"

"Before you and she fell in love?"

"Put it that way if you want to," Mears said. "I don't know. Perhaps—perhaps she had let him think—had even thought herself—what's so wrong about it, if she did?"

"Nothing," Bill said. "Nothing at all. Not about that. Mears—was he still trying?"

"Not getting any—" Mears said, and stopped again.

"But, still trying. Hadn't given up entirely. Miss Latham is a very attractive young woman—" Bill let it trail off, and waited.

"Sometimes it looked that way," Mears said, and momentarily seemed to speak to himself, to be unconscious of the man he spoke to. But then he straightened, and the flush came back under the tan.

"And did I kill him because I was jealous? And so she would get the money and we could have it? Or—did we do it together, somehow? That's what you're saying?"

"Well?"

"*No, damn it all!*" There was a dazed expression in his eyes. "We're not that kind of people," he said. "We wouldn't do a thing like that."

Which, of course, is a statement often made—with every evidence of shocked sincerity—to policemen. But not exclusively by those who are innocent of doing things like that.

X

THERE WAS AN unexpected reticence about The Breeders' Nook, which Pam thought of as a cat store. Miss Madeline Somers had seemed a hearty, youngish woman—a woman of the no-nonsense type, usually (at least by Pamela North) associated with dog people. But the shop, well up on Madison Avenue, on the ground floor of an elderly five-story building, had an air of reserve. For one thing, the name of the shop, lettered in the lower right hand corner of the plate glass window, was in small italics and without capitals. (Beneath the name, in even smaller lettering, *cats and cat supplies*.) For another thing, the only cat in the window was a ceramic cat; a reproduction of an Egyptian statue cat, austere and haughty, as becomes a god. One could assume, and Pam did assume, having paid off her cab, that Miss Somers's prices would also be austere and haughty.

But—there was a sign in the window which was somewhat less reticent. It appeared to have been lettered by an amateur. It read: "Special Sale. All Cats Drastically Reduced."

Encouraged, although faintly surprised, Pam North went down two steps at a little after ten on Monday morning and opened the door of *the breeders' nook*. A bell tinkled softly. Pam went into a carpeted room which, although small, contained several upholstered chairs. In the center of the room there was a pedestal with a wide top covered in white carpeting. The pedestal was empty; so was the room. Pam felt that she had walked unannounced into someone's living room and had an inclination to walk out again.

At the rear of the room was a wide, curtained, opening into the room beyond. There was no indication of cats or, indeed, of any life. But then, from behind the curtains, a Siamese cat spoke. Although reasonably familiar with feline Siamese, Pam was not certain what the cat had spoken of. Not, she thought, of breakfast. Pam started to speak herself; to say, probably, "Is anybody else home?" But she did not, because as the words formed in her mind, a man spoke from behind the curtains—obviously, from some distance behind the curtains. The man had a very high-pitched voice.

"—to make a final commitment," the man said. "Nevertheless—"

It was evident that he had begun the sentence elsewhere, presumably in a room beyond that which the curtains hid.

"I do believe," a woman said, in a much more robust voice, "that we have a customer."

Her remark put a period to whatever the man had planned to say further, qualifying his (apparent) declination to commit himself.

The curtains parted. Madeline Somers, wearing a beige-colored silk suit, came through them and said, "Why! Mrs. *North*" in a tone of marked cordiality. "You *did* decide to come."

"Yes," Pam said, and felt herself inadequately responsive. Perhaps, she thought, she should add something more. "Goody! Goody!" somehow seemed indicated.

"I've had you in mind," Madeline Somers said, coming fully into the room. "Very *much* in mind."

"That's nice," Pam said, rejecting, with a little effort, "The hell you have."

"I may," Miss Somers said, "I *just* may, have one you'll like. I—"

She was interrupted. A thin, pale-faced man came through the curtains. He wore unusually large spectacles; he had flat, pallid hair. He said, to Madeline Somers, "You'll let me know, then?" and the voice was the high-pitched voice. He looked at Pamela North and his lips twitched slightly, in what was, presumably and rather symbolically, a smile.

[104]

Pam was quite sure she had never seen the pale man. He, nevertheless, seemed somehow familiar. It was as if, she thought, she had read about him some place; as if he had walked off a page. For no reason she could lay mind to, she thought of Dickens. Uriah Heep? She had always thought of Uriah Heep as pale. Although not with heavy-rimmed glasses. Pecksniff? She could not think of Pecksniff at all.

"I'll call you," Madeline Somers said.

The pale man walked thinly past Pam and out of the shop. The bell which had tinkled her entrance tinkled his departure.

"Do sit down," Madeline Somers said, and indicated one of the chairs. "I'll bring the one I had in mind for you."

Pam sat and adjusted her mind. It was not, certainly, as she had expected. She had expected cages of cats. Or, perhaps, bins of cats. She had expected kittens biting the tails, worrying the ears of other kittens, and that one leaned over and, having said, "Aren't they cute?" according to ritual, said, "That one, perhaps?" and pointed.

Things were, obviously, not handled so at *the breeders' nook*. This was rather more like buying a dress, from an experienced saleswoman who had the very thing for modom and too much sense to confuse modom's ill-equipped mind with excess goodies.

"Really a darling," Miss Somers said, and just stopped, Pam thought, on the verge of adding, "little number." She went through the curtains. She returned, after a few moments, carrying a Siamese cat who wiggled in her hands and was told, in firm tones, to quit that, now. The cat voiced his (her) opinion of that injunction.

Miss Somers stood behind the pedestal and held the cat on it. She shaped the cat into a sitting posture. The cat said, "Wow-*ou!*"

"Isn't he a doll?" Miss Somers said. He was, of course. What three-months-old kitten is not a doll? "Look at this tail," Miss Somers said, in admiration, and bent the tail back over the young cat's back. It reached to his shoulder blades. He said, "Ur-*ah!*"

"Look," Miss Somers commanded and turned the young cat on his side, exposing his belly. "Not a *vestige* of a stripe. Not the faintest tabby markings." Miss Somers indicated the cat's flanks and sat him up again.

Pam had got up, approached the cat on display. He turned and looked at her, from deep blue eyes. A charming cat. Only—

"He's pointed," Pam said.

"Do you really think he's pointed?"

"Oh," Pam said, making amends, "not as much as some. Only—"

"*I* don't think he's pointed," Miss Somers said. "I really don't, Mrs. North."

("Of course it can be let out a little here. And taken in here, perhaps. But I really don't think, Mrs. North—")

"And," Pam said, "what we really have in mind is a female. Because whatever people say, males do tend to spread afterward."

"Oh," Miss Somers said. "You plan to alter?"

Her tone took a dim view of any such plan.

"We do," Pam said, firmly. "We bred Martini and the poor little thing—"

Damn it, Pam thought. I *won't* puddle up.

"I can," Miss Somers said, "give you a very special price, you know. You saw the sign in the window?"

Pam nodded her head. And, again, the feeling of faint surprise entered her mind. She could not imagine why. Then, she could. It wasn't anything—it was only that, met at the cat show, clearly seeking customers, Miss Madeline Somers had said nothing about having a sale of cats.

"All of them marked down," Miss Somers said now. "This one, for example. Seventy-five last week. I'll let you have him for fifty."

"It's very reasonable," Pam said. "I guess. Only—"

"*You're* the one who must be satisfied," Madeline Somers told her, firmly, settling that argument. "There is the most adorable little

[106]

female. Rather on the small size, but they should be, *I* think. And quite a *round* face. Wait."

She took the male away. She returned with a smaller cat. The new cat also wiggled and also spoke.

"Perfect accent," Pam said, gravely, and again Miss Somers blinked, and then laughed with what could be taken as appreciation.

The new young cat was another doll. Possibly, even more of a doll. That was agreed upon; the faintest vestiges of a stripe were admitted frankly. But since Mrs. North didn't plan to breed, or to show— And Mrs. North couldn't deny that the face was rounder. And, although this one, too, was listed at fifty—Pam had a feeling that Miss Somers consulted a price tag, although literally she did not—Miss Somers was willing to let her go at forty, considering that Mrs. North was Mrs. North. (Precisely what this had to do with it was not apparent, at least to Pam.)

"Already inoculated," Miss Somers said. "And papers, of course. And I assure you, not an *iota* of French."

(English and American Siamese fanciers consider French breeders somewhat overtolerant in certain matters.)

That, Pam explained, didn't really matter. What they wanted was merely a cat—a cat with familiar markings and well-known intonation. And, a rounded face. Which, admittedly, this youngster nearly had.

"A darling, really," Pam said, drawn to the young cat. But, not certain. "I'd want my husband to look at her before we decided," she said, feeling more than ever as if she were buying a dress. "I wonder if you could—er—hold her for a day or two?"

Miss Somers compressed her lips. She said, with doubt, "We-ll." Absently, she brushed her skirt with the palms of her hands. Pam recognized the gesture, and its futility.

"The trouble is," Miss Somers said, "and I haven't told very many

[107]

about this, but I'm selling out. This is really—well, call it a clearance sale."

Pam said, "Oh."

"So I can't promise," Miss Somers said. "You see how it is? If somebody comes along—"

"Of course," Pam said.

"The lease is due to expire," Miss Somers said. "And the rent they want for renewal!"

"Of course," Pam said. "But I'm afraid the earliest time my husband can—"

"And it's really time for me to retire," the sturdy woman in her late thirties said. "I've been thinking for some time that it's really time I—"

There was, Pam thought, certainly no reason Miss Somers should explain. "I—" Pam said.

"And," Miss Somers said, "these dreadful New York winters. I'm from California, you know—Los Angeles—and I just can't seem to get used to all this cold and snow and everything."

"I'm sure," Pam said, "that California must be very pleasant. If he can arrange it so we can both come in tomorrow?"

"Oh," Miss Somers said. "Tomorrow! That's a different thing. I'm sure she'll still be here by tomorrow."

What, Pam North wondered, tinkling her way out, is so different about tomorrow? So different as all that? And it *was* a little strange that Madeline Somers, if for some time planning to have a bargain sale of cats, hadn't mentioned the fact forty-eight hours or so before.

A little strange, Pam thought, waving at a cab. But not very interesting.

"Saks Fifth," she told the cab driver. Now that the subject had been brought to her attention—

The cab was making a right turn into Forty-ninth Street when Pam remembered. Not Uriah Heep, not anybody out of Dickens.

The man Jerry had told her about—the man with a manuscript, the antivivisection man. Of course—Gebby had said that Madeline Somers was a member of the Committee Against—oh yes, Against Cruelty. One of the crackpots. The man named—of course. Floyd Ackerman. Stopped by to crack a pot with Miss Somers, probably.

Pam tucked this minor recognition into her mind and said, to the cab driver, "This'll do," and paid and slid between the bumpers of parked trucks to the sidewalk and the Forty-ninth Street entrance of Saks Fifth Avenue.

***

Mr. Notson would see Captain Weigand now. "Now" was ten thirty Monday morning, and Bill Weigand had been waiting for fifteen minutes to be seen by someone of the firm of Cameron, Notson and Fleigel. He had waited comfortably enough on a leather sofa, with the opportunity to read *Harper's*, the *Atlantic Monthly* or, if his taste ran in that direction, *Reader's Digest*. He had spent the time turning his mind over, recapitulating for his own benefit.

Doug Mears had been, at least until nine that morning, in the inn at Forest Hills. For all Bill knew, he was twiddling his thumbs. There was a string on him—not too tight a string; it wouldn't hold if Mears decided to break it. If Mears tried to break it, that would be all right, too. They would know more then, and use something stronger. Hilda Latham was at her parents' home in Southampton. She was, if she heeded a politely worded request, waiting for Sergeant Mullins to come out and to help him clear up one or two points which had arisen. (Such as: Had she been engaged to John Blanchard and changed her mind on the appearance of a gangling, tow-headed tennis player? But not changed a normal interest in half a million dollars?)

One Floyd Ackerman had left his downtown, walk-up apartment at eight in the morning and had had breakfast in a nearby drugstore. He had then gone into the Independent subway station below Eighth Street on Sixth Avenue and disappeared from view. No great effort had been made to keep him in view. It did not appear that, at the moment, he was worth that many men.

Robert Sandys was being of what help he could to two detectives who, in the cavernous apartment on Riverside Drive, were going through papers, and Mrs. Sandys had made them coffee. Sandys had obligingly found a discarded tennis racket of his late employer's and one of the detectives—the taller of the two—had swung it in a service motion, and reported that the ceiling was high enough.

Captain Weigand would come this way, please. Captain Weigand went that way—went into a large corner office, with leather-covered furniture and a large desk. The man behind the desk, who stood up and came around it when Bill entered, was also large; he was white-haired, deeply tanned. He held out a brown hand. There was an outward innocence about Stuart Notson. He had, however, extremely shrewd blue eyes.

It was a hell of a thing about John Blanchard. It was a thing which was hard to believe. That good old John— And he—all of them—certainly wanted to do anything they could to help.

He sat down solidly behind the desk and Weigand sat in a client's comfortable chair, facing him.

Bill told Notson, in general, the provisions of the will they had found in Blanchard's apartment. Notson nodded. That, so far as he knew, was the last will. Only—

"Gave me a ring Friday," Notson said. "Made an appointment to come down today—would have been here about now—" He paused and shook his head, in recognition of this sad coincidence of timing. He had said he wanted to make a few changes in his will.

Bill Weigand raised his eyebrows.

"Old story, isn't it?" Notson said.

"Right," Bill said. "Cut somebody out? Or don't you know?"

"I don't know," Notson said. "Somehow, I doubt it." He put the first two fingers of either hand against firm cheeks and looked at Weigand. "This isn't evidence," he said. "My guess was—just a guess, mind you—that all he wanted to do was to change a little wording. Now it reads something like, 'To Hilda Latham, of Southampton, Long Island.' Maybe he wanted to change it to read, 'To my wife, Hilda.' See what I mean?"

"But—"

"Foresighted," Notson said. "I'm guessing. He'd been seeing a lot of the girl. Turned out to be a damned pretty thing, didn't she? Have the will got ready. Wouldn't need to sign it unless and until. Earnest of good faith, eh? And not any piddling little half million. The works, eh? Not that I say the girl's for sale. Still—with poor old Graham on the rocks the way he is. And John—well, John was quite a man. Older than I am, by a little. But—what's that, eh?"

Bill Weigand blinked slightly—and inwardly. He said he gathered that Mr. Notson had known John Blanchard rather well.

"John was a partner here, you know," Notson said, speaking to a man who hadn't known at all. "Cameron, Notson and Blanchard, it was. Left us about fifteen years ago, and we kept the style for a while and then Abe came in. And poor Joe Cameron died— This hasn't anything to do with what you want, has it?"

Anything might have. Bill Weigand couldn't know in advance. Had Blanchard, since, been practicing law? On his own? With another firm?

He had not. Oh—now and then something came along. He was, for example—had been until the day before, anyway—the court-appointed administrator of the estate of an old friend of his. "Of mine, too. And that's a funny thing. You'd think—"

What Bill Weigand would think was that a man like Alex Somers, who had had brains enough to earn himself a fortune, would have had sense enough, too, to leave his affairs in order when he died.

Which had been about two years ago. "Particularly when he spent most of his time flying around in company planes," Stuart Notson said. He shook his rather distinguished head. "Didn't even make a will," he said, in despondent disbelief. "Trouble for everybody. And some relative he'd probably never heard of—" The big man shrugged heavy shoulders. He looked sharply at Bill Weigand. "You made your will, captain?"

"Yes," Bill said. Something tugged at his memory. Nothing in his memory gave.

"Good," Notson said. "Aside from things like that—the surrogate's a friend of his, but everything was according to Hoyle—John didn't work at the law. Didn't need to, obviously. Spent a lot of time on tennis committees, things like that. Played a bit of bridge. Wrote a bit, just for the fun of it. Crazy about cats. Funny thing for a man to be crazy about, isn't it?"

"I don't know," Bill said. "A good many men are, apparently. A friend of mine—"

He found he was in danger of being diverted. He put himself back on the track. He said Mr. Notson had mentioned bridge.

"Very good at it, John was," Notson said. "Tournament caliber. Could have been top flight if—I suppose if the cats, and tennis, hadn't taken so much of his time."

Notson had played with John Blanchard frequently. Usually at Blanchard's apartment, sometimes elsewhere. Often with Graham Latham as one of the four. Latham was good, too. If he had as much savvy about other things as he had about bridge, poor old Graham would be a lot better off.

"Tell me about Graham," Bill said. "I gather you know him fairly well?"

"Classmates," Notson said. "He and poor old John and I—all the same class at Princeton. After that, John went to Columbia Law and

I went to Virginia and Graham—well, Graham began to make those investments of his. Poor guy."

"Poor?" Bill repeated. "Is he?"

"Comparatively," Notson said. "I feel as if I were gossiping over the back fence, captain. Not supposed to blab in my trade." He paused. "Of course," he said, "Graham isn't one of our clients."

"Mr. Notson," Bill said, "in my trade we listen to a lot of gossip. If it hasn't any bearing—"

The captain was not to think that Stuart Notson didn't realize what he was driving at. So—all right—

Graham Latham had been born to a lot of it—and to a big house in Southampton and things that went with a lot of it, and big houses anywhere. If he had been brighter, or more indolent, he would have let it go at that. But—

His father had been a—call it a financier. He had made most of what he left Graham Latham in the market. "Easier in those days," Notson said. "Before SEC. Easier to lose it too, of course." Graham Latham had decided to show everybody—"to show himself, I guess" —that he was as good a man as his father had been.

"And," Notson said, "he wasn't. A thoroughly good Joe. But didn't have the knack. And wouldn't admit it. So now—well, now he's got a big house and a lot of grounds and—you live in the city, captain?"

"Yes."

"Then you don't know what it runs to, keeping a place up," Notson said. "We've got a place up in Connecticut. Not a patch on Graham's. Keeps us broke keeping the grass cut." He paused. "In a manner of speaking," he added.

As to what, in detail, Graham Latham had left of what he once had had, Notson didn't know. It wasn't one of the things, obviously, you asked about. And people could be "poor" on a variety of incomes. He didn't for a moment suppose that the Grahams went hungry. But—

[113]

"It's very relative, of course," he said, and now seemed more thoughtful than before. The legal mind was there, Bill decided. "And to a degree it's—well, the entire shape of a man's life. If you're brought up one way—the way I was. Perhaps the way you were, captain—it's one thing. If you grow up as Latham did, it's quite another. And—you get saddled with things. Like that place of his. Theoretically, it's worth a lot of money. But—to whom? That's the question. Hundred thousand. Hundred and fifty thousand. Hell, I don't know. Cut the land up in one-acre plots—fine. The money rolls in. And the zoning board lands on you. Offer it whole, as an estate—I suspect Graham has, although he's never said so to me—and—" He shrugged. "Like having a yacht for sale," he said. "When all anybody wants to buy is a cabin cruiser. Meanwhile—taxes and keeping the grass cut. We're getting a long way from John Blanchard, aren't we? And who killed him?"

"Miss Latham is—close to her parents? Would want to help? If, by the standards she's been brought up with, she thought help was needed?"

He was, Stuart Notson said, being asked to be a mind-reader.

"Not," he said, "that I can't read yours, captain. On this point, anyway. About the girl—she's a nice girl, captain. From all I've ever seen. Probably, a responsible girl. As I said, I can't picture her marrying anybody—I know what you're getting at—just for the money. But, John was quite a guy. I said that, too. Good looking, vigorous—hell. A good many women have found it easy enough to fall for John."

"Oh?"

"His wife died a good many years ago. Just before he left the firm, as a matter of fact. What would you expect, captain? John was no plaster saint."

"Right," Bill said. "I get your point. A very understandable—compromise—it might have been. All around. Only—"

"Only," Stuart Notson said, "John got killed."

"Right," Bill said. "However, I was thinking more of something else, Mr. Notson."

This time Notson said, "Oh?"

"I'm afraid," Bill Weigand said, "that Miss Latham fell in love."

Notson said "oh" again. He said it flatly, this time. He said, "Afraid, captain?"

"As you said," Bill said, "Mr. Blanchard probably wasn't a saint. It would be very generous of him, wouldn't it, to leave half a million dollars to a girl who'd dropped him to marry somebody else? Saintly, you could almost call it, couldn't you?"

XI

SERGEANT MULLINS drove the police car, which was not marked as such, along a narrow blacktop road, as he had been told to by a man at a filling station, and kept his eyes open. The sign was of wrought iron and read "Graham Latham." He turned on the driveway, through the gap in the stone wall. Iron gates which might have stopped him stood open. The drive wound through lawns, among trees. The drive, Mullins thought, could use a few loads of gravel. The grass could stand cutting. Nevertheless, all very plush.

When the drive made its last turn but one, Mullins could see the house. A large house—in fact, a tremendous house. A brown shingle house, in front of which the drive circled. There was a porte-cochère and Mullins stopped the car in it, and walked up two wooden steps —which could have done with a coat of paint—to a white door. He pressed the button and, distantly, inside, a bell rang. He waited, briefly, and a man answered the door. The man said, "Morning?"

He was a wiry man of medium height, with gray hair in a brush cut and a crisp gray mustache. He was deeply tanned. He had unexpectedly full red lips and the faint, conceivably encouraging, smile behind which he waited showed very even, very white, teeth.

"Miss Latham?" Mullins said. "If she's in? My name is Mullins. Called earlier—"

"Right you are," the wiry man said, and pushed the screen door toward Mullins. "Anything we can do." He shuttered the faint smile. "About poor Johnny, of course." He shook his head slowly. "Bad thing," he said. "Damn bad thing. Come along in, eh?"

[116]

Sergeant Mullins went along in—went into a large, square hall, walked on a worn carpet.

"I'm Latham," the wiry man said. "Hilda's father, y'know. Tells me you and some captain gave her a bit of a going over."

His tone made light of this.

"Walked into it a bit, didn't she?" he said. "Not that I mean into it, of course. In here, if you don't mind. She'll be along any minute."

They went into a room off the hall. It was a large room, with a large fireplace at the far end, with french doors along one side. Two of the doors were open, behind screens; they opened onto a terrace. A rather weedy terrace.

"Too early to offer you anything, I expect," Graham Latham said and then, his voice raised, "Hildy? Your visitor's here." He directed this information through the open french doors. Apparently from some distance, a girl said, "Coming."

"Cigar?" Latham said, and Mullins said "No thanks." Latham moved—moved well, moved quickly—to a table and opened a box and took a cigar out of it, bit off the end, lighted the cigar. The cigar was appropriate to his face, Mullins thought. Cigars aren't to many faces. Latham wore a blue polo shirt and walking shorts and blue stockings which stopped just below his knees, and the clothes, too, were appropriate, although the man probably was nearing sixty. He didn't look it, Mullins thought. He'd kept himself in good shape.

Hilda Graham came from the terrace into the room. Yellow gladioli trailed from her left hand. She wore slacks and a loosely fitting sweater, and was a girl who could wear slacks. She said, "Good morning, sergeant. With you in a minute," and to her father, "Last of them, I'm afraid," and then she went on across the room and out of it on the other side, into the hall. She came back quickly, without flowers. "Had to put them in water," she said. "Now, sergeant?"

Mullins looked at Graham Latham, briefly. "Don't mind if I sit in," Latham told him, did not ask him. But he was pleasant about it. "Watching brief," he said, and added, "as they call it. Eh?"

"Why not?" Mullins said, assuming there was nothing, in any case, to be done about it. Mullins had worn a blue business suit. It felt a little stiff on him. "Won't take long," Mullins said.

"Sit down, sergeant," Hilda Latham said, and herself moved to a chair. The deep red hair swayed as she moved. Quite something, she is, Mullins thought. And knows it. And why not? She sat down and leaned a little forward in the deep chair. The chair's dark slip cover was somewhat worn. "That's right," Latham said. "Take your choice, sergeant." Mullins took his choice. He chose a straight chair, and sat squarely in it.

"One or two points," Mullins said. "Captain Weigand thought you could clear up, maybe."

"Like," Mullins said, "did you know Mr. Blanchard left you half a million dollars, Miss Latham?"

The girl's eyes widened; she looked startled. She looked at her father, who sat up straight in the chair he had been comfortable in and said, "My God!" He looked at his daughter for some seconds. He said, again, "My God," and there seemed to be wonder—conceivably admiration—in his voice.

"No," Hilda Latham said. "I—are you sure?"

"Yeah," Mullins said. "That's what the will says. You didn't know?"

She shook her head, the dark hair swaying.

"Good old Johnny," Graham Latham said. "My God."

But, as he looked at Sergeant Mullins, waiting, his eyes narrowed somewhat. The crinkles at the corners of his eyes were the crinkles many smiles leave behind them. He was not, now, smiling. He was, Mullins decided, considering.

"It seemed," Mullins said, "like a good deal. To the captain, that is. He sort of wondered whether you had expected anything like that. Seems you hadn't."

"Not like that," the girl said. "Certainly not—half a million *dollars*?"

"Uh-huh," Mullins said.

"Of course," Latham said, "poor old Johnny hadn't kith or kin. There's that, sergeant. And he's always been fond of Hildy. Avuncular, y'know." He looked at Mullins. "Like an uncle," he said.

"Sure," Mullins said. "And he never said anything about leaving you money, Miss Latham? Didn't even sort of hint?"

"No," the girl said. "Oh—I wouldn't have been surprised to get something. He was generous. And, as daddy says, there wasn't— wasn't anybody really close. But—as much as that!" She shook her head again.

"That's the point," Latham said. "Something—yes. But— My God!"

And then, as if involuntarily, he looked around the big room. He surveyed it, Mullins thought, as a householder; as a householder who saw blemishes. And who, now, could look at them without pangs.

"What would you have expected?" Mullins said. "Just at a guess, Miss Latham? Under the circumstances?"

They both looked at him. There was a rather long pause. It occurred to Mullins that they did not want to rush into anything. Or even to edge into anything.

"What do you mean, circumstances?" Hilda asked, and her father looked at her quickly. Sharply? Because, in her voice, there had been a note of wariness, of defense.

"Why," Mullins said, "like you said—both said. The circumstance of feeling toward you like an uncle." He paused and looked at them slowly. He managed to look surprised. He also looked formidable. "What did you think I meant?" he said, slowly.

"That's right," the man said, and was quick. "That's all we—"

"Not," Mullins said, "the way a man would feel toward a young woman who meant a lot more to him than—than a niece? A girl as pretty as you are, Miss Latham? A girl who had a key—"

Latham stood up, the movement abrupt.

"I don't like that," he said. "Don't like any part of it."

"Well," Mullins said, and did not move. "Sorry about that, Mr. Latham. What don't you like?"

"The implication. That Hildy would—" He did not finish that. "You'd better get out of here, sergeant."

"Sure," Mullins said, and did not move. "I could do that. Will if you want to make a point of it. Come back with some of the local boys. Then we can all go into town and have a nice cozy little—"

"Daddy," the girl said. "You're giving the sergeant—" She hesitated. "The wrong idea," she said. "That we've got anything to hide. That—"

The wiry man looked down at her. Something, Mullins thought, passed between them. Almost as abruptly as he had stood up, Latham sat down again. He said, "Sorry. Got the notion you—" And shrugged.

"O.K.," Mullins said. "Maybe I put it the wrong way. Miss Latham—did Mr. Blanchard want you to marry him? And did you say, maybe, that you would, maybe? And then did you meet this Mears fellow and—"

Latham moved as if to stand up again, and the girl took charge. She said, "No, daddy," and then, "there isn't anything—wrong about it. Nothing to be—ashamed of."

She turned to Mullins, then.

"I suppose," she said, "there are dozens of ways you could have found out. How doesn't matter. Yes—Johnny did ask me to marry him. And—I was fond of him. There wasn't anybody else. Then. Nobody he didn't make look like—like a small boy. And—"

"Hilda!"

Graham Latham leaned forward in his chair as he spoke his

daughter's name, stopping her. He repeated the name, as sharply as before.

"You're talking too much," he said, when she looked at him and waited. "The sergeant here isn't—it's not any of his concern."

"I—" the girl said, and at the same time Mullins, in a much heavier voice, said, "We-ll—."

"Well," Mullins said, "I wouldn't say that, Mr. Latham. We're interested in all sorts of things. You'd be surprised what interests us. And then, Miss Latham, this fellow Mears came along? The one you said yesterday was—whadja say? A kid, wasn't it?"

"Hilda!" her father said again, again with command in his tone. But this time it did not stop her.

"All right," she said. "All right, Sergeant Mullins. Doug came along. This kid came along."

"Yeah," Mullins said. "And so you told Mr. Blanchard all bets were off? And he said—what did he say, Miss Latham? That it was O.K. with him?"

"Of course," she said.

"Sure," Mullins said. "Said for you to go right ahead and that he thought you were doing the right thing and all like that. Didn't make any—pitch?"

"He understood."

"Sure," Mullins said. "An understanding man. When did you break it to him, Miss Latham? Yesterday, maybe?"

"I—" she said, and hesitated. "Yes, yesterday. But—I think he knew before. Things like that—I think he knew before. Or guessed." She looked at Mullins, then, with her head raised. "I'd never told John that I loved him," she said. "He—he didn't ask me to."

"He didn't try to talk you out of it? Not any?"

Scepticism was in Mullins's voice. It was put there with care.

"No," she said. "Oh—he said I must be sure it wasn't—wasn't just something I'd get over. But as to talking me out of it—" She shook her head, and the deep red hair swirled.

"Sergeant," Latham said, "are you a gossip columnist? On the side?"

"No," Mullins said. "Just a cop, Mr. Latham. A cop wondering about things. Whether, maybe, Mr. Blanchard would have been quite so generous if your daughter, after she'd had time to think it over, had said, finally, that she was sorry and it was no soap. Might have cut half a million down to—oh, his grandmother's ring. The one with a topaz in it." Mullins looked at the tanned man who didn't look his age. He looked steadily. "Dead men can't do any will changing," he said. "Where were *you* yesterday morning, Mr. Latham? Here with your daughter—you *were* here yesterday morning, Miss Latham?"

She nodded her head and looked at her father. And waited. Her greenish-blue eyes seemed to Mullins to narrow just perceptibly as she waited.

"What the hell business—" Latham said and then, suddenly, his full lips parted in a smile and he said, "Sorry, sergeant. Silly thing to say. Particularly since I was going to tell you, as soon as we got around to it. I was in town night before last. Playing bridge."

He paused, evidently for a question. Mullins did not ask the question.

"With poor old Johnny," he said. "And a couple of other chaps, of course."

He waited—waited as a man might who expected what is called a double take.

He got none. Mullins said, "Well," in a voice of mild interest.

"Until about midnight," Latham said. "And—at Johnny's apartment, sergeant."

"Hmm-mm," Mullins said. "And then—I take it you didn't drive back here that night, Mr. Latham? It's quite a drive."

"No. Stayed at the club. The Princeton Club. Left early and drove back home before the traffic picked up. Got here about—oh, well before noon."

"Uh-huh," Mullins said. "Left about when, Mr. Latham?"

Somewhere around eight, Latham thought.

His daughter had left to keep her luncheon engagement in Forest Hills before he arrived?

"Yes," Hilda said, answering for both of them. "I drove in in the bug."

"One of these days that bug of yours is going to fall apart," Latham said. "All together and nothing first, like the old chaise, eh? Only, the way things are now, we'll be able—" He caught himself becoming cheerful, apparently. He said, "Poor old Johnny. Hard to believe he's gone." He sighed.

It was hard to believe a good many things, Mullins thought, half an hour later, beginning the long drive back. He'd turn a lot of things over to the loot and see how he made out.

***

Jerry, seeing his wife waiting in the Algonquin lobby, debated briefly whether he would be the conventional husband of folklore. He decided to leave the comic-strip personality to those of comic-strip mind. Going up to her, smiling down at her, he said it was a very pretty new fall suit and that he assumed she had been able to walk right out in it.

"I had a bet with myself," Pam said. "I bet you would. I won. I'm glad you like it and I could and it wasn't at all expensive, considering. After lunch, could you take time to look at a cat?"

If they didn't take too long over lunch, Jerry said, as they went into the Oak Room.

"She's really a bargain," Pam said, as they sipped. "More than the suit, to be honest. Marked down from I don't know what."

"To?"

"Forty dollars," Pam said. "Admittedly, she has what some people might call a stripe. But on the other hand, she's not pointed. Not as they go. She puts them on a pedestal. One at a time, of course."

That took some explanation, over corned beef and cabbage. Jerry agreed that it was an odd way to sell cats and that he, too, would have expected a bin. He said he supposed it came under the head of merchandising.

"Packaging, really," Pam said, in the taxicab bound, slowly and tediously, north. "The poor little things. Probably it would have been quicker to walk. But I had to get new shoes, too, to go with the suit. You didn't notice them, incidentally."

It is Jerry North's opinion that women set far too high a store on shoes, and that one pair of shoes looks, on the whole, very like another. He said they were very pretty shoes and went beautifully with the suit.

They walked down two steps to the door of *the breeders' nook*. There was a shade pulled down on the door. The shade had one word lettered on it. The word was "Closed."

"Well," Pam said. "She was certainly quick about it."

That, also, needed explanation. Pam explained on the way downtown. She said that Miss Somers looked rather young to retire— particularly between ten in the morning and— "What time is it now?" It was two thirty in the afternoon.

"Between ten and two thirty," Pam said. "But I suppose once a person decides—" She became silent. Jerry waited.

"Nothing," Pam said. "Except that Saturday she didn't say anything about having a cat sale and if she wanted to sell cats you'd think that would be the first thing to mention, wouldn't you? And this morning, even, she would be selling cats for a few weeks, and certainly tomorrow, when we were supposed to go in. Before I thought of our having lunch together, of course."

[124]

"Of course."

"Which may," Pam said, "be all she's gone to, and there was nothing to indicate she had an assistant. Did I tell you your Mr. Ackerman was there this morning?"

She had not. She did. She said that, of course, Gebby had said that she, which was to say Madeline Somers, was also a member of the bunch of crackpots, which was to say The Committee Against Cruelty. And that Ackerman had probably gone around to get a contribution or something. And that—still? Did Jerry think?

Jerry would, he told her, think that she was making bricks without straw. Or, for that matter, clay.

"Nothing to tell Bill, then?"

He doubted that Bill would be interested to hear that Miss Madeline Somers's cat store was closed, possibly for lunch. Or that Floyd Ackerman had been at the store that morning. If Pam was sure it really was Ackerman. And—

"Another thing," Pam said. "About Gebby. Of course it doesn't mean anything, but—"

"Mac," the cab driver said, "I can't stand here. The cop's looking at me already, and he's one of the mean ones."

They were in front of the building in which North Books, Inc., has offices. Jerry said, "I'll try not to be late," and Pam, "Keep your flag down. I want to go to—"

As the cab continued south, Pam told herself, again, that, of course, it didn't mean anything. Only—Dr. Oscar Gebhardt, cat specialist, was, often had said he was, entirely opposed to hospitals for cats. He had not had a hospital for years; he operated on cats in his office on Park Avenue, he brought cats home, still unconscious, for convalescent care; he regarded hospitals as very bad for cats, who thrive best in familiar surroundings and known hands, who also are subject to infectious diseases which may sweep through a cat hospital.

What did not mean a thing was that he had, apparently, sung another song to John Blanchard—a song in praise of a research center which was, nevertheless, to be at least partly a hospital for cats, among other small animals. And been left a considerable sum to—to orchestrate his song.

"Not Gebby," Pam told herself, firmly, as she paid the hack driver, remembering that the city tax was part of the fare, not part of the tip.

"It's perfectly ridiculous to think that Gebby—" Pam told herself in the elevator and checked her mind.

It is not, of course, in matters of this kind, *perfectly* ridiculous to think of anything.

XII

GERALD NORTH dictated.

"As you know," he said, "the fifty-fifty division between author and publisher in the proceeds of book club sales is a long-established practice and one which—" He paused, and the hurrying pencil waited expectant in the hand of Miss Abigail Clark. "We'd better cut out 'long,' Miss Clark," Jerry North said, overcome by honesty. Miss Clark's pencil searched, found, eliminated. "Since book clubs are after all rather recent," Jerry said, in needless explanation. This was in the not-dictating tone and the pencil continued to wait. "—is essential to the economic structure of the industry under present conditions," Jerry said. The pencil moved. "In other words," Jerry said, "we like money too." Miss Clark smiled; did not make notes. "Therefore—" Jerry said, and the telephone rang.

"Yes, Janey?" Miss Clark said. She listened. She said she'd see. She said, "It's that Mr. Ackerman. The one with the—"

"Good God," Jerry said. "*No!*"

"Mr. North is—" Miss Clark said, and stopped to listen. Jerry could hear the quick rattle of Jane Lester's voice. "Well," Miss Clark said, "I'll ask."

"Jane's going nuts," she said. "He's called three times and she's used the in-conference one, and the just-stepped-out one, and the can-you-call-him-back one. And hung up. And he's called back in the next breath and—"

"Good God," Jerry said, and reached. He said, "Yes?" in something like a snarl and then, "Oh, sorry, Janey. Put him on." Then he said,

"Yes?" again, but could not quite recapture the snarl. A snarl wasted, he thought, and listened to a high-pitched, excited voice.

"All right," Jerry said. "I was in conference. Then I stepped out. Listen, Mr. Ackerman—"

Floyd Ackerman did not listen.

"It is essential," Ackerman said, "that I see you at once. Essential." His speech was redolent of capitalization.

"I'm afraid—" Jerry said.

"Or," Ackerman said, "the Responsibility will be yours." His voice trembled, approached falsetto.

"I'm afraid," Jerry said, "that our decision is final, Mr. Ackerman. No doubt some other publisher—"

"Not that," Ackerman said. "Not about that. I realize your position. The Pressures. I am resigned. About this man Blanchard."

Jerry said, "Oh."

"Exactly," Ackerman said, and his voice shook. "Exactly. There's no time to waste. No Time. I have something to tell, something Vital. And—there's danger. Do you hear me? *Danger!*"

Jerry removed the receiver a half inch from his ear.

"Listen," he said. "Will you listen a moment? You have information about Mr. Blanchard's—death?"

"How many times—"

"Give it to the police," Jerry said. "They're the ones—"

"Corrupt," Ackerman said, and his voice was even higher than before. "Inefficient. Ride rough-shod. The third degree. You think I don't know?"

"Yes," Jerry said, "I certainly think you don't know. What have you got to tell?"

"Enough," Ackerman said. "But—don't talk about the police. They're part of the whole thing. Don't you understand?"

Jerry didn't.

"They'll crucify me," Ackerman said, and there was increasing

[128]

hysteria in his voice. "I wouldn't have a *chance*. You think I don't know that?"

The man was, Jerry thought, irrational—now entirely irrational. And—frightened?

"All I want is a chance," Ackerman said. "Just a chance. But—*you're against me too!* I can tell that. You and all the others. I'll give you half an hour. I can't wait any longer than that."

"I don't—" Jerry said.

"And if you bring the police," Ackerman said—almost screamed. "If you bring the police, you'll never find me. None of you. I'll tell you and then—I'll go then. Know a place. Until—until it's safe. I've got a right to stay alive."

It made, obviously, no sense. There is little point in telling a man who is hysterical, who has gone over the final edge, that what he says—what he screams—makes no sense.

"Of course you have," Jerry said, and tried to make his voice a soothing voice; tried to get understanding sympathy into his voice. He made a decision. "All right," he said. "Come here, then. We'll—talk it over. I promise until we do I won't—"

"You must," Ackerman said, "think I'm crazy."

There was no immediate answer possible to this. It was clear that merely saying "Yes," would be of no help.

"You've got my address," Ackerman said. "Haven't you got my address?"

"I suppose so," Jerry said, and covered the receiver and said, to Abigail Clark, softly, "Ackerman's address?" She nodded.

"Yes," Jerry said, to Ackerman. "But—listen. What you're asking is—"

"Come—" Ackerman said. "*Go* there. I'll leave it so you can get in. If you're alone—alone, you hear? *Nobody else.* You hear me?—if you do what I say I'll join you as soon as I'm sure and—we'll see. If you—if we can work out some way I can have a start—then—"

It seemed to Jerry that, although now the shrill trembling voice was lower, Ackerman was losing even the coherence of his irrational purpose. It was as if, even while he talked, the man—the thin, pale man with staring eyes behind thick lenses—were disintegrating. Suddenly, Jerry could see him, telephone in his hand, shaking through all his thin body in a kind of desperation—

It was preposterous; it was, in a sense, enraging. *"Hold this,"* something was saying, something implacable, grotesquely unfair. And thrusting into Jerry North's resisting hands—what? A thing that ticked, that might go off. It occurred to Jerry suddenly that what had been thus unfairly thrust into his hands might be a man's life.

"I'll come," Jerry said. "Wait." He paused for a second. "Wait!" he said and made the word heavy, as if he set it as a block, an anchor, to hold a slipping mind.

Within seconds, looking at the replaced telephone, Gerald North was telling himself that he was a fool. A man—a crackpot—had something to tell which was probably of no importance and was frightened into incoherence—on the edge of which he always trembled—by, it was almost certain, a threat which had no existence. And I, Jerry thought, a steady businessman—or as steady as my particular business allows—have been stampeded into—

But then the shrillness in the voice, the something near desperation in the voice—in the voice itself, more than in the tumbling, unrevealing words—sounded again in Jerry's ears. Whether it made sense or not, the man was frightened—the man was scared to death. And as that worn phrase came into his mind, Jerry stood up. It occurred to him that, in some manner entirely obscure, Floyd Ackerman might be just that.

It was not until he was in a cab, bound downtown, with certain things tidied up, certain instructions left for Abigail Clark, that a somewhat more likely possibility entered Gerald North's mind. Those most likely to be in fear of the police, and to want to run—to "have a start," are those who have specific reason to fear the police. Among such, of course, murderers are prominent.

The thought was slightly chilling. It did not, however, add any rational note to the unreason of the whole business. If Ackerman had decided to confess to murder he was certainly going about it in, even for him, an odd fashion.

Of course—and this thought occurred as the cab finally—traffic had been very heavy—turned east off Fifth, below Fourteenth, and went into an area which is a conglomerate of almost everything—of course Floyd Ackerman might be inviting one Gerald North into a trap. Gerald North could not think of any reason why he should be trapped. It seemed unlikely that, although Ackerman had certainly resented the rejection of his book, he had resented it quite—well, quite that much.

Unless, Jerry thought, as the cab stopped in front of a four-story building, once a private house, now either tenement or apartment house, Floyd Ackerman merely liked to kill people who—call it criticized him.

Anyway, Jerry thought as, having paid off the cab, he climbed the stoop—anyway, I'm bigger than he is. In the dim vestibule, he bent to examine name cards above mailboxes, push-buttons. It appeared that Floyd Ackerman lived in the third floor apartment; it appeared there was one apartment to each floor.

Jerry pushed the appropriate button and waited for the inner vestibule door to buzz at him. It did not and he pushed the button again. Then, remembering, he tried the door. It was not locked. Ackerman had said he would leave things so that Jerry could get in—get in and wait for him.

Jerry climbed the first flight of stairs. It occurred to him, as he neared the top, that John Blanchard, also, had been bigger than Floyd Ackerman—bigger and, certainly, stronger. The thought was not encouraging.

Jerry climbed the second flight of stairs to the landing and on the landing faced a door. He knocked on the door and waited. Nothing happened. He tried the knob, and it turned and he went into a hallway which connected two large rooms—a hallway off which opened a bathroom and a small kitchen. The arrangement was familiar; the Norths have lived on floor-through apartments in converted houses; in apartments of two large rooms, connected by narrow halls. The living room, presumably, would be on the street side. Jerry called Ackerman's name, at first softly, then more loudly, and was unanswered. He went through the hall to the living room.

The big room was comfortably furnished. There was nobody in it. There was, apparently, nobody in the apartment. So— Floyd Ackerman was behaving as he had planned. Some place—outside the building? More simply, one flight up in the building?—Ackerman had hidden himself to watch, to wait until he was sure that the man he had summoned had come alone. Jerry looked at his watch. It was a quarter after four. Give the jittering little man ten minutes.

Ten minutes was long enough to spend on this—this charade. It seemed, now, to be no more than that—the frightened voice had dimmed in Jerry's memory. A rather silly charade for a grown man to be engaged in, particularly during working hours. It occurred to Jerry that there was one more possibility—it could be that he had been had. The purpose was obscure, but no more obscure than anything else. To get him here, out of the way, while somewhere else something else was done which required the absence of Gerald North? He could not think what was elsewhere to be done. After all, Ackerman had only got him out of his office. It was improbable that Ackerman—it was certainly Ackerman who had called—planned some action in the offices of North Books, Inc.

The hell with it, Jerry thought, and sat down in one of the comfortable chairs. Give him the ten minutes—no, now the seven minutes. Leave a note saying he had been and gone. Go. And—

[132]

Dimly, he heard footsteps outside—footsteps on, evidently, the flight leading down from the floor above, then on the linoleum surface of the outer corridor. So—Ackerman had waited above, peering down; now was coming—

He was not. The footsteps did not stop at the door to Ackerman's apartment. The door did not open. The footsteps diminished, now, on the flight below. Another tenant, going about his business—probably her business. Going out, probably, to get a pound of coffee, a loaf of bread. Apparently, Ackerman had lurked somewhere in the street, and so would come up the stairs when he came. If he came. Five minutes—four—the hell with it. Ackerman was taking too long, far too long, to assure himself that the police had not been brought. Do now what he should have done long ago—call Bill, tell him about this charade, take the raised eyebrows, the regretting sound made by teeth and tongue, that he had earned.

Jerry got up, walked through the hallway to the other large room, the bedroom, at the rear of the apartment. Conceivably, Ackerman might have fallen asleep. Or, succumbed in some fashion to his own excitement.

The large bedroom—also well furnished—was empty. Somewhat absently, Jerry looked into a closet—a large closet. Clothes hung neatly in the closet. Shoes were neat on the floor. Ackerman was not in the closet. Why on earth should he be in the closet?

All right—having gone so far in a fruitless charade, make sure. Jerry went back into the hall and opened one of the two doors. The door opened into a bathroom. Nobody in the bathroom.

Jerry tried the other door—the kitchen door.

Floyd Ackerman was in the kitchen. He was hanging, straight, neat, his feet six inches from the floor. He was hanging by the neck on a length of thin rope—actually, a very heavy cord—which had been hitched around a thick pipe which ran across the kitchen, just below the ceiling. A small stool lay on its side on the floor, just out of reach of the dangling feet. He was wearing his glasses.

If Floyd Ackerman had had a right to live, he had elected not to exercise it further.

Jerry found a knife in a kitchen drawer and cut the body down. The action would not, he supposed, be approved, but it was inevitable. He could not leave the thin little man, who would never shake again—never raise a shrill voice again in hysteria—dangling grotesquely there. He touched the body as little as he could, lowering it with hands under armpits. He did not touch the tipped-over stool and did not tamper with the knots.

There was warmth in the body. Dead now—Jerry made as sure of that as a layman can—Ackerman had not been dead long. He could not have been—it had not been long, not much more than three-quarters of an hour, since he had talked on the telephone, and talked in fear. He must have killed himself almost at once after Jerry North had said, so slowly, so carefully—so ineffectually—"Wait."

It made no sense. There was no use trying to guess sense into it. The telephone was in the living room. Jerry went into the living room.

***

By a little after four on Monday afternoon it began to look that, as a suspect, Graham Latham had what it took. Mullins was, admittedly, pleased with this; he had brought Latham back as a suspect, more or less on a silver platter, and Weigand, listening, had said "right" several times before they got at it—by telephone, through the cooperation of precinct detectives. They had been lucky.

That Latham had a motive as good as any, and better than most, leaped to the mind. Half a million dollars in a daughter's name is half a million dollars in the family—in a family which, obviously, could use it. Between Latham and the money there was little chance that whim might intervene. "The girl might change her mind about this guy Mears," Mullins pointed out, pointing it up. "Not about daddy." Latham impressed Mullins as a tough guy—tough mentally and physically. The girl—Mullins wasn't so sure about the girl. Sorta nice, the girl seemed to be. So—

Latham had played bridge with Blanchard and two other men, at Blanchard's apartment, the night before Blanchard died. The two other men, reached at their offices by telephone—for once things broke smoothly—had agreed to this. There had been nothing unusual about the bridge game—Latham had won fifty dollars or so, but there was nothing unusual about that. "Be a hell of a lot better off if he'd played cards instead of the market," one of the men said. "Good old Gray." The game had ended around midnight, because Blanchard had to get up early to go to Forest Hills.

Latham had stayed overnight at the Princeton Club, precisely as he said, and had left early—around eight—also as he had said. "Plenty of time to have dropped by to knock Blanchard off on his way home," Mullins pointed out, and Bill Weigand said, "Right, sergeant."

He would have had to "drop by" after Mears had left, if Mears was telling the truth. He could have been there, with Blanchard dead, when Ackerman rang the doorbell—if Ackerman was telling the truth. "Wouldn't say, 'Come on in, lookit what I've just done,'" Mullins pointed out.

"Give him a ring," Bill said. "Ask him, nice, if he'd like to come in and give us a little more information. And—get the locals to stand by."

But the luck ran out, then. Mrs. Graham Latham—answering the telephone in Southampton in a crisp voice which carried the accent, the intonation, of good New York—was sorry, but her husband was not in. He had gone to the city. Nor was Hilda in. She was playing tennis at the home of friends. Why, yes, she thought Mr. Mears was one of the players. But she hadn't, certainly, queried her daughter as

[135]

to that. She was sure that her husband, when he did return, would be glad to get in touch with Sergeant Mullins. She was sorry that she did not know where, in the city, he could be reached.

The "locals"—but actually the State police—would keep an eye on things and, if it seemed indicated, provide transportation into town for Mr. Graham Latham. When—and of course if—he showed up.

"Pretty sure I didn't scare him off," Mullins said. "Of course—if he got worried—"

Bill doubted it.

"Could be," Mullins said, "he's come in to start shopping."

"Right," Bill said. "Could be he has, Mullins." He drummed his desk with active fingers.

They had, of course, only a theory—call it, at best, a probability. They hadn't placed Latham in, or near, the apartment house on Riverside Drive. Without that—

The telephone rang. Mullins answered, said, "O.K., Mr. North," and handed the receiver to Bill Weigand, who said, "Yes, Jerry?" And listened. And said, "The hell he has," and, "Wait for us." And hung up.

"Floyd Ackerman's hanged himself," Weigand said.

"The hell he has," Mullins said. "That's a hell of a note."

He spoke in sorrow. He had been rather pleased with the contents of his silver platter.

"Of course," he said, "it don't have to mean—"

He did not finish. His heart was not in it.

"Jerry North walked in on him," Bill said.

"Damn," Sergeant Mullins said. "They sure make things screwy, don't they?"

[136]

XIII

Pam's first thought had been of Jerry, and of the shock it must have been to him to find Floyd Ackerman dangling from a pipe. Jerry agreed it had been but, after a second drink, added that he would live through it. Unlike Floyd Ackerman.

"The poor man," Pam said. "Why? I suppose because he killed Mr. Blanchard and—and what? Remorse? Or merely fear that he would get caught?"

Jerry could not help her, except by guessing. He had thought Ackerman, talking on the telephone, was a man afraid. Certainly he had indicated that he was a man about to run. But, instead, he had killed himself. Bill might know more, when he came.

They had finished dinner, then, and were waiting for Bill Weigand. When the police had arrived at Ackerman's apartment, Jerry North had told his story once, and told it briefly. Bill had said, "Right, you want to wait here or shall I come around?" Jerry had had no desire to wait there—wait in the way of technicians; wait while the thin body of Floyd Ackerman, dead by strangulation—dead, grotesquely, with his thick-lensed glasses on—was taken away.

Jerry hated to think of the glasses. It was not quite clear why they had added a final macabre touch—except that, when he had opened the hall door, the light had caught the lenses and been reflected from them, so that, for a hideous instant, the dangling man had seemed to be winking at Jerry North—winking as if they shared a secret between them. When he had finished remembering this— and not telling Pam about it—Jerry had had another drink.

It was almost nine when Bill came. He came alone; he looked

tired. Always, they could tell how long Bill had been at it, and to some extent how it went, by the tiredness in his face. He looked, now, as if it had been going on for some time, and not going well. But when Jerry let him in, and raised enquiring eyebrows, Bill said they had found nothing to indicate that things were not as they appeared to be—that Ackerman had not killed himself.

He was offered a drink and took coffee, instead. He listed, briefly, the facts which did not contradict appearances.

The stool was where it would have been if Ackerman had stood on it, pushed it away when he was ready. The noose around his neck had been made by tying a bowline in the rope's end and forming a loop by running the line through the bowline's eye. In effect—in all that chiefly mattered—it had been a hangman's knot. The other end of the rope had been passed twice around the pipe, and made fast. The thick pipe, left exposed as so often happened when the building was remodeled, had been more than adequate to support Ackerman's light weight. It appeared that Ackerman had left some slack, but not enough for the purpose, which would have been to break his neck. So—he had strangled.

He had left no note. As often as not, they left no notes, especially when the decision came suddenly and the action, afterward, was almost immediate. The cord he had used was three-eighths of an inch in diameter (and hence had cut deeply into the man's thin throat) three-ply, brown, natural fibre. More simply, it was such a strong cord as is frequently used to tie up heavy parcels. Ackerman might have received such a parcel and saved the cord—conceivably for the use to which he had finally put it; more probably for any use which might crop up. He might at some time have bought the cord to tie up some heavy parcel he was shipping—a box of books to someone, for example. The cord—or thin rope if they preferred—would have supported the weight of a much heavier man than Ackerman.

It was possible, of course, that he had gone out and bought the cord after making up his mind, which presumably would have been after his telephone conversation with Jerry. Which brought them back to that. So—

Jerry went over it again, trying to remember, trying to quote. It had not been coherent.

"Right," Bill said, when he had listened. "You thought he was afraid? Of us—of the police—chiefly? That he wanted to tell you something and—run. Why you?"

"I don't know," Jerry said. "We'd met. I suppose he could have heard that we've been—mixed up in things like this. But I don't know."

"You told him you'd come? Asked him not to do anything until you did? Promised not to call us in?"

In effect—yes.

"You should have had more sense."

Jerry knew he should have had more sense. He had done this much—he had told his secretary to call the police if she did not hear from him within an hour.

"The only thing," he said, "Ackerman said he would be watching. Would hide if the police came. I believed him. And—he sounded scared, Bill. Scared to death."

"He was," Bill said. "Apparently he was. You waited—how long?"

Jerry had waited in the apartment almost exactly ten minutes before he went into the other rooms, before he found Ackerman hanging. He—

He stopped suddenly.

"Bill," he said, "if I'd looked earlier—found him earlier?"

"I doubt it," Bill said.

"But you don't know?"

"I don't know. You saw nothing to indicate there had been any-one else in the apartment?"

Jerry North shook his head slowly. And Pam, sitting beside him on a sofa, put her hand over his, pressed his hand. "All right," Jerry said. "I—" Again he broke off, and now looked at Bill Weigand, looked intently.

"I told you," Bill said. "Everything is consonant with suicide."

"Even the glasses?"

"He could see almost nothing without them, the M.E. says. Judging by the lenses. He would—well, he would have needed them to tie the knots."

"Speaking of the knots," Pam said, "what's this one you call a bowline? I never heard of it."

Bill told her, as well as the shape of a knot can be told without demonstration.

"He'd know how to tie one?" Pam said. "It sounds—complicated."

Sounded more than was, Bill said. He smiled suddenly, and weariness ebbed from his face. He said that if she was looking for some special person—a sailor, perhaps? If so, they had nothing to indicate that Ackerman had ever been a sailor.

Pam said, "Really, Bill. Although I did see a movie the other evening—one of the old ones? On TV? And there everything depended on a man's tying a square knot. A *square* knot. Even I— don't I, Jerry?"

"At least half the time," Jerry said, with gravity, but felt better, with Pam back. He thought of mentioning the laws of chance, but decided against it.

"All right," Pam said. "Forget knots. Bill—you say 'consonant' with. A—a careful word?"

"A detective should always be sceptical," Bill said. "Says so in the manual. But—no cigarettes still burning, Jerry? No faint odor of perfume?"

He spoke lightly. He sounded serious. Jerry North shook his head.

"Nothing heard? No distant closing of a door? No window eased down?"

"Nothing," Jerry said, "except somebody going downstairs. Somebody I first thought was Ackerman, coming down from where he had been hiding. Only— Probably just somebody going out to market. Anyway, no pause outside Ackerman's—" He stopped abruptly. He was being looked at hard.

"My friend," Bill Weigand said, "it took you quite a time."

Jerry looked at him blankly.

"To remember the footsteps," Bill said. "Oh—I can see they wouldn't have had any meaning. Unless, Jerry, you knew that the floor above Ackerman's—the *only* floor above—is unoccupied. Nobody lives there, Jerry. Nobody goes down from there to the corner grocery."

There was rather a long pause. Jerry dented it, slightly and after some seconds, by saying, "we-ll." And then Pam, with some reproach, said, "*Jerry!*"

"Man or woman?" Bill said, and Jerry—feeling now a little put upon, and that this was not his day—shook his head. He said he couldn't be sure. He had at first thought the footsteps those of Ackerman himself. So he could not, obviously, have been sure they were those of a woman. But, subsequently, he had explained them—with the fraction of his mind available to something of so little importance —as the footsteps of a woman on her way out to buy food for dinner.

"*Jerry!*" Pam said.

Jerry said he was sorry. He said that, at the time, he had not known Ackerman was dead.

"A *murderer*," Pam said. "Only a wall away. And you just—sat there."

"Hold it," Bill said. "Hold it, Pam. There's no evidence—"

"Killed the poor little—man," Pam said, evidently having rejected "crackpot" out of deference to the dead. "Made it look like suicide.

[141]

Heard Jerry coming. And—*Jerry. Don't tell me you rang the bell?*"

"I'm sorry," Jerry said. "I guess you didn't bring me up right, dear."

"You," Pam said. "And, since he couldn't come down, because you were coming up, went up and waited and—*really,* Jerry."

"I'm *very* sorry," Jerry said, doing what little he could to strengthen it. He looked at Bill Weigand.

"Right," Bill said. "It's possible, obviously." He smiled, however. If there was faint tolerance in the smile, Jerry preferred not to notice it.

"Is there anything else you two haven't got round to passing on?" Bill Weigand said.

"I can't think of any—" Jerry began, but again Pam said, *"Jerry!"* Jerry stopped, obediently.

"Miss Somers," Pam said. "I said we ought to. That she—"

But this time Bill Weigand interrupted. He said, "Somers?" Then he said, "Damn. You did mention her before and I—damn!"

They waited.

It was nothing, he told them. Almost certainly nothing. That morning, while he had been talking with a lawyer named Notson, something had tugged at his memory and nothing in his memory had responded. Now he knew what had tugged—a name. The name of Somers; a name repeated. One Alex Somers, dying intestate; Blanchard his administrator. One Madeline Somers, keeper of a cat store. Presumably it meant nothing; was one of those coincidences which plague life, and investigations. Still—what about Miss Somers?

They told him of Miss Somers—of her revelation to Pam, that morning, that she was about to go out of the cat business and back to Los Angeles; the suggestion, by no means conclusive, that she had gone out of business very suddenly, and closed the shop. (Although at least one potential customer had undertaken to return.) It wasn't,

Pam admitted, much to go on. Miss Somers might merely have gone out to lunch—a rather late lunch.

"Or, of course," she added, "gone out to deliver a cat. I do hope she didn't sell Winkle."

They both looked at her. They looked at each other.

"Nothing definite," Pam said. "It just—came into my mind. That if we bought her—the little queen—we might call her Winkle."

"Why?" Jerry asked, and made it simple.

"She felt like Winkle," Pam said. "Don't always ask me why."

"All right," Jerry said. "Gladly."

"It's subject to change," Pam promised him. "And we don't even know if we'll get her. We want to look at her again. Tomorrow, probably. Anyway— Mr. Ackerman was there this morning. I'm almost sure it was he. Just as Jerry described him. If you're trying to make a check on his movements." She paused. "By there," she said, "I mean at the cat store. With Miss Somers. Not that it means anything. At least, we thought it didn't." She paused again. "While he was alive, that is," she said, finishing it off.

"Buying a cat?" Bill said. "Or—or what?"

"Now," Pam said, "how would I know. You want me to intute?"

"By all means."

"He said something about would she let him know, and she said she'd call him. So I supposed, something to do with the Committee against whatever it is. Probably, a contribution, because Gebby says she was one of them."

Bill said, "Hm-mm." He said, "Tell me about the place, Pam."

She told him—a showroom; behind it, cut off by curtains what was—probably—well, call it a stock room. Where the cats are kept. Beyond that, she thought, another room—probably an office.

They waited.

"I was only in the showroom," she said. "But she came back very quickly with the cats, so I thought the next was where they kept

[143]

them. And she and Mr. Ackerman—I'm sure it was Ackerman—apparently had been in still another room, and I supposed the office. Where she keeps her checkbook. Does it make any difference?"

Bill considered. He said it probably didn't. As a matter of fact—

"As a matter of fact," he said, "it could clear up—or maybe fog up—one point. The suit Ackerman was wearing—a dark gray flannel—had recently been cleaned. Smelled of cleaning fluid. But—there were cat hairs on it. Fore and aft. No cats in his place. No cat hairs on the furniture, except one or two which might have come from his clothing, rather than the other way around. If he visited this shop—there would have been cat hairs to be picked up?"

"Wherever there are cats," Pam said. "They do it all the time. Summer and winter. What kind of cat's hairs?"

"Siamese, the lab boys think."

They had assumed that Ackerman had got cat hairs on his clothing in Blanchard's apartment, where it was to be assumed cat hairs abounded. Now, obviously, the assumption needed modification. He could have picked up cat hairs at the cat shop. Most probably, by sitting on a chair where a cat had sat.

"As," Bill said, "I ought to know."

"Not any more," Pam said. She looked around the room. "Not any more," she said again. There was, for a moment, nothing said. "All right," Pam said herself. "I won't let myself. You said, 'fore and aft'?"

"Back of coat," Bill said. "Seat of trousers. And—front of trousers."

"Of course," Pam said. "He sat on a chair a Siamese had been on and then—then put the cat on his lap and—"

She stopped. Bill had narrowed his eyes, apparently in doubt. He did not actually shake his head, but shaking of the head was somehow implied.

"It's possible," he said, in a tone which suggested the absence of the word "barely." "Or, he may have brushed against something, I suppose. The point is—he didn't like cats. Tried to kick one of Blanchard's."

"Why the—" Pam said, and stopped. "Missed, I hope?" Jerry said, "The cat take appropriate counter measures?"

"Dodged," Bill said. "Hissed. Probably would have swished if he'd had anything to swish."

"Oh," Pam said, "a Manx. I do think cats ought to have tails, but I suppose it's their own business. You mean, he wouldn't have taken a cat on his lap. Some people are very strange. How, then? Because it's very difficult to sit on your own lap. I mean—"

She had, Jerry told her, put it very well.

"Bill," Jerry said, "what you really think is he was murdered. Strangled—strung up when he was unconscious. By the person who —who heard me coming, went up another flight out of sight until I'd gone into the apartment, went back down again after the coast was—damn."

There was no use going on worrying about that—about a thing which was no more than a possibility.

"Which sure needs explaining," Jerry said, still morose, self-blaming.

"To do that," Pam said, and spoke slowly—"to strangle him, and hold the body up and—hang it up—a person would have to be strong, wouldn't he?"

"Right," Bill said. "At any rate, reasonably strong. But, actually, Ackerman weighed very little. And once the cord was over the pipe —well, it's easier to pull down than to lift."

Pam nodded, to show her comprehension of the mechanics of the matter.

"But still," she said, "have to hold him up—move him around— come in contact with him?"

"Right," Bill said. "And if the murderer had cat hairs on his clothes, some of them would come off on the victim's clothes—Ackerman's clothes. His suit had texture, would pick up hairs."

"And," Pam said, and spoke even more slowly, "all at once Miss Somers closes up shop and—*Bill!* She's one of the heirs of this Somers this lawyer told you about and somehow—" She stopped. "Only," she said, "how? And why, for that matter?"

And Bill Weigand, this time, did shake his head.

"We've got a much better one," he said. "Graham Latham. A man who needs money. And who now, through his daughter, gets money. And—I haven't told you this—spent part of Saturday night at Blanchard's apartment, playing bridge. And—Blanchard's apartment is an ideal place to pick up cat hairs, including the Siamese. I did myself, and Mullins did and—"

The telephone rang. "The North answering service," Jerry said, and went to answer. He said, "O.K., sergeant," and Weigand went to the telephone. He said, "Right, Mullins," and for some seconds listened in silence. Then he said, "Right, morning will do," and added that he'd be in his own apartment in half an hour or so, and that Mullins might, also, go and get some sleep. He hung up the receiver.

His face was not tired any longer. His face was satisfied.

"Latham called in," he said. "We'd asked him to come to town to fill in a few gaps, give a few more details. Called to say he'd be glad to, but would tomorrow do? Because—because it seems Mr. Latham has sprained his back and driving is rather uncomfortable with a sprained back, and there aren't any more trains tonight. Sprained it lifting something, he says."

"Lifting?" Which was Pam, getting it straight as straight.

"Right," Bill said. "Lifting. It's the usual way."

"Back instead of knees," Jerry said, in a voice of experience. "Lifting what?"

"Mr. Latham," Bill said, "thinks it must have been a chair. Says

[146]

the pain came on slowly, and he did lift a chair this morning and—he can't think of anything else he did lift."

He smiled, rather contentedly.

"Perhaps," he said, "we'll be able to jog his memory."

XIV

"Take nothing for granted—investigate and be convinced," reads
the Manual of Procedure of the Police Department of the City of
New York. Bill Weigand reminded himself of that at his desk Tues-
day morning. Get minor things cleared away, while waiting for
the arrival from Southampton of the major "thing"—Mr. Graham
Latham; while waiting to be told, in more detail, how Mr. Latham
had sprained his back, if not by hanging up a man; while waiting
to ask Mr. Latham whether he had not, while at Blanchard's apartment Saturday night, got cat hairs on his clothes; to ask, further, if
to Saturday night they could not add Sunday morning?

It would be pleasant if Mr. Latham, confronted by what they
had, would dissolve into confession. Mullins, who had seen him,
thought this unlikely, and Bill Weigand places considerable reli-
ance on Sergeant Mullins. Pleasant—but, then, improbable. Hence,
the slow business of filling in was going on elsewhere; the slow,
careful business of asking people who had no part in any of this
whether they had seen any part of it. If they could find somebody
who had seen a man answering Latham's description going into the
apartment house on Riverside Drive, or coming out of it, that would
be fine. If somebody had noticed a man who looked like Latham in
or near the converted dwelling in which Floyd Ackerman had died,
that would be equally fine. Either one would be enough.

It would be better, obviously, if Latham could be placed at the
scene of Blanchard's murder. Broken on that, Latham might be willing to tell them why he had killed Floyd Ackerman. Merely to
supply the police with an alternative murderer, and one who could

not talk, could not deny? Bill rather doubted it. It would imply, for one thing, that Latham knew enough about Ackerman to know his feeling toward Blanchard. There was no reason to think he had, no way to prove—

Bill checked himself. Blanchard might himself, at some pause in the bridge game, have mentioned Ackerman and his Committee Against Cruelty; might have given Latham enough to go on. Another thing to ask Latham, when he came.

More likely, Bill thought, half his mind on the papers he was glancing through, Ackerman had been the somebody they now sought—the somebody who could place Graham Latham at the Blanchard apartment. It might be that Latham was the person Ackerman had seen getting out of the elevator. Bill thought he had seen somebody, and had lied about it for reasons of his own—the most likely being a chance of future profit. (To be spent, quite possibly, to further the campaign against animal research, the end justifying the means.)

Implicit in that assumption—that suspicion—was the further assumption that Ackerman had known Latham by sight and had known, further, that there was a relationship between Latham and Blanchard. Otherwise, obviously, a man leaving an elevator in a large apartment house would have been anybody—nobody—to Floyd Ackerman, and not worth a second glance. Another thing to ask Latham—would Ackerman have known him by sight? (Not that, under the circumstances, a very revealing answer was to be expected.)

Waiting, Bill Weigand continued to look at papers selected from the filing case of the late John Blanchard. "Anything that might conceivably have bearing," had been the instructions. The two men working in the apartment had allowed a good deal of latitude. Most of the documents—letters, receipted bills, bank statements—Bill skimmed provided only general information about John Blanchard.

The chief information provided was that Blanchard had had at least as much money as he had thought he had, and that a large part of it was in stocks. (And fifty thousand plus in a checking account, presumably available for incidentals.)

No threatening letters; no demands for immediate payments or else; nothing to indicate, offhand, that John Blanchard had not led a most uneventful and circumspect life until somebody had hit him over the head with something. (Tennis racket? Cat-scratching post? Something else not yet guessed at?)

A few papers which seemed to be connected with the Somers estate of which Blanchard had been administrator. Copies of a final audit, finished some two months before; the originals presumably in the surrogate's files. Another healthy estate, apparently—almost as healthy as Blanchard's own. Receipts for certain court-authorized expenditures. A carbon of a letter to Miss Madeline Somers, of —— Madison Avenue, stating that distribution of the estate might be expected to commence early in the following year. A letter reading: "In response to your letter of the fifteenth, this will authorize you to expend the sum of twelve hundred dollars ($1,200) for a marker for the grave of Cousin Alex" and signed "Madeline Somers."

This was dated from —— Madison Avenue on August 30 of that year. Indicating, Bill thought, that Miss Somers had then been accepted as, at the least, one of the heirs of the late Alex Somers— "Cousin" Alex Somers. The letter had been twice folded, to fit envelopes of differing sizes. So what? And—

The telephone rang. "Right," Bill said. "Bring him in, sergeant."

Bill pushed the few remaining papers to the back of his desk and put a weight on them. Mullins brought in Graham Latham, who wore a dark gray suit and a worried expression. He also walked stiffly and, when he accepted the invitation, sat down stiffly. He also said, "Ouch."

"Nasty things, back sprains," Bill said. "How'd you do it, Mr. Latham?"

Latham started to shrug his shoulders, winced, and gave that up. He said that the only thing he could think of was that he had moved a chair the previous morning—a not especially heavy chair. He hadn't noticed anything for some hours, but that happened often enough. The chair was the only thing he could think of. Bill made a suitable tck-ing sound. He said, "Mr. Latham, did you know a man named Floyd Ackerman?"

Latham repeated the name, as one repeats a name heard for the first time. Then he said, "No." Then he said, "Captain. Can you tell me anything about my daughter? About Hilda?"

"About her?" Bill said. "What do you mean, Mr. Latham?"

The compact tanned man looked at Weigand for some seconds before he answered. Then he said, "She's not here, then? Or—somewhere else? What I mean is—she's not under arrest?"

"No."

"Or—detained for questioning, eh? You know what I mean, captain. Any way you want to put it."

"I know what you mean, obviously," Bill said. "No. You mean, you don't know where she is?"

"That's it," Latham said. "Went to these people for tennis. The Bensons. Had a drink or two afterward, and changed, and said she had a dinner date and drove off in that bug of hers. And—didn't come home last night. Didn't call up. Not like her, captain. Her mother's no end worried." He paused. "I am myself," he said, and looked it. "Not like the girl. Not like her at all."

It seemed a side issue. But, at a guess, Latham's anxiety was authentic. (At a guess. Without committing the mind to anything.) If so, a block for the moment in Latham's mind. Clear away the side issues, so far as that was possible. At least, display a sympathetic interest. Bill displayed one.

The Lathams had discovered their daughter's absence when she failed to appear for breakfast. "Don't keep her on a lead, y'know," Latham said. "Comes and goes as she likes. Responsible sort of kid." Mrs. Latham had gone to her daughter's room; found that her daughter's bed had not been slept in. She had called the Bensons, and discovered when Hilda had left and that she had left alone, mentioning the dinner engagement. Latham had telephoned the inn at Forest Hills, seeking Doug Mears—and had learned that Mears had checked out the night before.

"The hell he had," Weigand said. "He was supposed—" He did not finish. Others had also been "supposed," including the local police to make periodic checks. "Go ahead," Bill said. "Then?"

Then they had called the State police, and discovered that, while there had been the usual number of motor accidents the night before, there had been none which resulted in death or serious injury, and none involving Hilda Latham, by name or by description.

"So I thought, 'By God, they've picked her up,'" Latham said. "And caught the next train in. And—you say it wasn't you?"

"No," Bill said. "You want to report her missing, Mr. Latham? Officially? To the Bureau? By the way, she's of age?"

"Yes. Just. I—she'd be sore as hell if she'd just—oh, decided to drive into town. Spend the night, eh? And we report her missing and the papers—" He stopped, seemed to consider. "Hold it up a bit, eh?" he said.

"Right," Bill said. "I would, I think. Now—"

"What's this about some chap named Ackerman?" Graham Latham said. "Eh?"

"The late Ackerman," Bill said. "Hanged himself yesterday afternoon. Or— You say you never knew him?"

"Never."

"Or heard of him? Blanchard didn't mention him?"

"Blanchard? No." He partly closed his eyes. "No," he repeated. "I'm sure he didn't. Blanchard knew him?"

"At least by reputation," Bill said. "Knew of him. Wrote a letter —you don't read the *Times*, Mr. Latham?"

"Sure I read the *Times*. What about the *Times*?"

"A letter," Bill said. "Printed Sunday. Written by Mr. Blanchard. Attacking an advertisement run by a group Ackerman headed—an antivivisection group. Annoyed Ackerman."

"No," Latham said. "What's this got to do with me, captain?" He was not belligerent in tone.

"Mr. Latham," Bill said, "when you were at Blanchard's apartment Saturday night. Playing bridge. Did you get cat hair on your clothes?"

Latham opened his eyes widely; his full lips parted. He said, "Now what the hell?" He blinked his eyes. He said, "I sure as hell did. Always did. Everybody did."

"Right," Bill said. "You like cats, Mr. Latham?"

"What the—" Latham said. And shrugged and winced. He'd sprained his back, all right, whatever else he had done. "As a matter of fact," he said. "I do. Did you bring me in here from Southampton to find out if I like cats? O.K., I like cats."

"Is that the suit you wore Saturday night? At Blanchard's?"

"Yes." And Latham looked down at the suit. His right forefinger and thumb snapped at his trouser leg. "You never get them all," he said. "And that Amantha cat, especially. Siamese cat. Friendly little tike. Sheds all the time. Thought I'd got them all."

"When? I mean, when did you brush your suit? Think you got all the hair off?"

"Sunday morning. Listen—what *is* all this about?"

"You're sure you brushed your clothes Sunday morning?" Bill said. "Not, say—last night? Or the first thing this morning? Or—"

"Listen," Latham said. "What's the use of asking me questions if

[153]

you don't believe the answers? Eh? I told you Sunday. How many times?"

"All right," Bill said. "This is what it's about, Mr. Latham. Perhaps Ackerman hanged himself. Say, because he was the one who killed Blanchard. But perhaps somebody strung him up to make it look that way. Strung him up because he knew something—maybe had seen somebody in the wrong place."

"So," Latham said. "That's where I come in? My daughter inherits a lot of money. You know by now we can use some money. Where else do I come in? And, for God's sake, where do cats come in?"

"There was cat hair on Ackerman's clothing," Bill said. "Siamese cat hair. His body could not have been handled without considerable physical contact. His suit was rough textured. A rougher texture than, for example, the one you're wearing. Cat hairs might rub off a suit like yours, Mr. Latham. Adhere to a suit like his. If you—"

"So," Latham said. "So that's it."

"Right. That's it."

"I didn't know this Ackerman," Latham said. "He wouldn't have known me. Wherever he'd seen me. And, he couldn't have seen me Sunday morning at Blanchard's place because I wasn't there. So, I didn't hang him. Or strangle him or whatever, eh? Does that cover it?"

"Right," Bill said. "You cover the ground. Where were you yesterday afternoon, Mr. Latham?"

"In town. You know that. Called up to—I suppose to tell me to come here. Had lunch with a friend at the Harvard Club. Can't say much for the food, but there you are, eh? Business friend. Partly on business."

"Right," Bill said. "At four o'clock yesterday afternoon. Say three thirty to—say four thirty. Still with the friend?"

Latham's eyes narrowed somewhat, presumably in thought.

"You don't have to tell me anything," Bill said.

[154]

"The old song and dance," Latham said. "Eh? Right to counsel and the rest of it. Nearly as I can remember, I was having a drink at the Commodore bar. Could be, two drinks. I drink scotch. I wasn't with anybody. I didn't see anybody I knew. About five o'clock, I got the car out of the Hippodrome parking garage and started home. I went downtown and took the tunnel. Didn't kill anybody on the way, captain. Must be slipping, eh? Whole—"

"Right," Bill said. "You've made your point. So, you won't mind dictating a statement? Covering—let's say covering everything, shall we? Starting with Saturday night. When, I gather, the cat named Amantha sat on your lap. Including when you brushed—"

The telephone rang. Bill picked it up and said, "Weigand" and then, after a moment, "All right. He's here," and held the telephone out to Graham Latham and said, "Your wife, Mr. Latham." Latham said, "Yes, dear," and listened and said, "Read it again, will you?" It appeared that she read it again; it appeared to be brief. Latham said he'd be damned and that there wasn't much they could do, was there? Weigand could hear the rustle of the transmitted voice. "Oh," Latham said, "some silly notion they've got. Nothing to worry about" and then, after a momentary pause, "No, I don't think it will," and "goodbye, then," and replaced the receiver. Bill waited.

"Wire from Hilda," Latham said, without being prompted. "Sent from Kansas City. Says she's on her way to California to marry Doug Mears and not to worry and that they barely made the plane. Apparently that's to explain why she didn't call before she—" He shrugged again, and the twitch of his face again made it clear he wished he had not. "So," he said.

"You don't," Bill said, "seem particularly surprised."

Latham said he was not, except by the timing. Both he and his wife had seen it coming—seen marriage coming. "Not this fast, I'll admit," Latham said. "But, kids move fast now, don't they? Figure

[155]

they haven't too much time, eh? Could be right, you know. No sense in wasting—"

He stopped, suddenly, as if he had tripped over something. He looked across the desk at Bill and his eyes narrowed. He looked away quickly, but not quickly enough. Bill guessed.

"It's true," Bill said, "that husbands and wives can't be compelled to testify against each other. Can't be called by the state unless they want to be."

"Now what?" Latham said.

"I thought that that had—crossed your mind," Bill said.

"Mears is an all right kid," Latham said. "A little apt to fly off—" He stopped himself.

"Right," Bill said. "I gathered that. And, of course, he'll have a rich wife. Unless—"

"You're crazy," Latham said. "First me. Now—"

"Unless," Bill said, "he killed to make her rich."

"You mean—if he killed him—and I'm sure as hell he didn't because—anyway, you mean if he killed Blanchard she doesn't get the money?"

He went to the point Bill had thought he might. Bill Weigand's voice nevertheless held surprise, simulated, when he said that he hadn't really meant that. If Hilda Latham—perhaps by now Hilda Mears—was not a party to the murder, her inheritance would not be stopped.

"All I meant," Bill said, "was that their married life might be—call it shortened, shall we? Of course, if she *was* in it—"

Graham Latham stood up at that; stood up too quickly and for a moment held on to the chair, steadying himself, pain in his face. A sprained back can hurt like hell, Bill thought. However one sprains it. But it was not pain that made Latham flush red under his tan.

"*If you try to lay it on my kid—*" Latham said, and his voice was suddenly hoarse. "*If you—*"

[156]

"Right," Bill said. "Take it easy. You'll what?"

He waited, and Latham looked down at him, glare in his eyes. But the glare faded slowly.

"See that you don't get away with it," Latham said.

"How?"

"In any way necessary," Latham said. "You want that statement you were talking about?"

For answer, Bill picked up the telephone, said that Mr. Latham wished to dictate a formal statement, suggested a room and a stenographer be found, waited briefly, said, "Right," and put the receiver back. "Sergeant Mullins will fix you up," he said.

"After I've finished?"

"I'll decide that," Bill said, "after I've had a look at the statement. Right?"

Mullins opened the door, and Latham went with him. Latham walked stiffly, with elaborate care.

He might, Bill thought, go a good way to clear his daughter—if he decided she needed clearing. On one hand, he might lie for her. On the other, of course—on the other he might tell the truth for her. It would be interesting to read the statement, Bill thought. More interesting than to continue through the papers taken from Blanchard's file cabinet—an unlocked cabinet, as it had turned out. One does not expect too much from unlocked file cabinets. Still—

Odds and ends. Surprisingly little to do with anything of any apparent importance. If there were documents which would shed light where light still was needed, they were not, it began to appear, in the files in Blanchard's apartment. Bill shuffled papers. It was difficult to understand on what basis the men at the apartment had made their selection. Presumably, on the assumption that the most perilous sin is that of omission—that it is safer to pile high than to overlook; best to buck decision to superiors.

Why, for example, had they thought the brief letter Bill now held

[157]

in his hand had conceivable bearing? A letterhead—stark, a name merely. "Paul M. Flagler." A date—the previous Friday. A letter, to John Blanchard.

"Dear Mr. Blanchard: You are quite right in your suspicion and proof should offer no difficulty. Actually, there are more discrepancies than resemblances, and I will so testify if necessary."

It was signed in a swirl in which, it was to be assumed, Mr. Flagler's name was somewhere hidden.

He would have saved himself time, Bill thought, if he had kept Nate Shapiro on at the apartment. Nate, with his customary gloominess, his unlimited capacity for self-doubt, nevertheless had the courage to decide. Nate would not have sent along this meaningless letter merely—well, presumably, merely because it *was* meaningless and so—

And Bill Weigand felt his mind caught as if in a noose, a choke collar. Paul M. Flagler. *Flagler*. *Of course!* The handwriting man. The consultant on disputed documents. The expert witness in courts of law.

Bill read again the brief letter from Flagler, who had obviously been consulted, to John Blanchard, who had asked a question. And, presumably, submitted a questioned document—and got his answer. The letter told him no more on second reading than on first. Bill put it down, and looked at the wall opposite and drummed on desk top with quick fingers.

It came to him slowly; he checked it slowly. There was not a great deal to go on, certainly; not much to build with. In the nature of things, there wouldn't be. The nature of things arranged. He went quickly through the papers, seeking something he did not expect to find—making sure he had not overlooked. He made sure.

He picked up the telephone, then. He dictated a message, urgent, to the police department of the City of Los Angeles.

When he had finished with that, he got an outside line and dialed a familiar number. He waited some time—some time after he had realized that a telephone was ringing in an empty apartment.

There was no reason, Bill Weigand told himself firmly, why he should find that fact disquieting. No reason at all.

He looked at his watch. The time was ten thirty-five.

XV

AT BREAKFAST, Jerry had said that it was out of the question—entirely out of the question. What with one thing and another, including time out to find a man hanging, he had, on the day before, got practically nothing done. He said that there was a great deal to do—people to see, letters to write; if possible, even manuscripts to read. He said that Simpson was, again, making noises about his contract, as he always did when an option ran out, and had even spoken dourly about Doubleday.

"Is he good?" Pam asked, diverted. "Because it's never seemed to me—"

"He sells," Jerry said. "Ours not to reason why. And it isn't as if you needed me. I have complete confidence in your judgment."

"Buck passer," Pam said, fondly.

"Anyway," Jerry said, "when they're little ones, what's there to go by? The way they look and—well, the way they look. It's later that you find out who they are. And who they are is partly who you are, anyway."

"Sometimes," Pam said, "you're not as clear as you might be."

"Association," Jerry said, and finished his coffee. "But you know what I meant."

"Of course," Pam said. "All right. It's left to me, then. I may decide no, and get me to a cattery. And, of course, the cat store may really be closed for good."

"Ummm-m," Jerry said, muffled by the closet into which he spoke while reaching for a topcoat.

"Don't try to drink Simpson into a contract," Pam said.

"Umm-m," Jerry said, and kissed the top of her head, which was the most convenient, in passing. And went. That had been at only a few minutes after nine.

Pam had another cup of coffee and another cigarette and what remained of *The New York Times*. What remained was the second section. A three-column cut of two lion cubs, wrestling at the Bronx zoo, dominated the split page—a very gay and amusing picture, Pam thought. They must remember to go to the Bronx zoo some day. The day, probably, otherwise devoted to the Statue of Liberty.

On the same page, below the fold, the passing of Floyd Ackerman, the well-known crusader against vivisection, was noted briefly —noted as a suicide by hanging. The police had, obviously, suggested no alternative. There was no connection made between the deaths of John Blanchard—Blanchard's death still commanded a corner of page one—and Floyd Ackerman. The *Times* had slipped there, Pam thought, and that was unusual for the *Times*. Presumably, the city desk did not read the letter column.

Pam went inside the second section. Danzig had a piece about Blanchard—a piece reviewing his services to amateur tennis, which were clearly many. Amateur tennis had suffered a loss.

Pam did not doubt it. She slipped from the sports pages deeper into the *Times*. The *Times's* man Stanley—no, Stanley was somebody else's man. The *Times's* man Shanley had looked at Maxwell Anderson's *Winterset* on TV and found it "stilted language in drab surroundings." Well! A very young man, Mr. Shanley must needs be; a young man with a tin ear. Pam sternly reminded herself that it takes all kinds, and cleared the breakfast table. She rinsed what needed rinsing and stowed in the dishwasher. (Pamela North likes to have things neat for Martha, who arrives at noon or thereabouts —arrives to make things neat. Jerry has spent no little time on this, and spent it fruitlessly. "Martha's so nice," Pam says, "and I don't want her to think we're sloppy.")

Dressed—in the new fall suit, the need for which had been somewhat indirectly brought to her mind—Pam looked through her purse for the card of *the breeders' nook*. She did not, of course, find it—not in the first purse or in the second. She turned to the Manhattan telephone directory, and found the number she wanted and dialed the number. The ringing signal was prolonged; finally the telephone was answered. "Breeders' nook," the voice said, and Pam reset the words in italic type. Pam said, "Miss Somers? This is Pamela North."

"Oh," Madeline Somers said. "Yes?"

She did not, Pam faintly felt, sound this morning like a very up-and-coming saleswoman. But Pam, having been married long to Jerry, makes allowances for morning moods. Pam, herself, feels fine of mornings.

"I'm so glad you haven't closed," Pam said. "When my husband and I stopped by yesterday there was a sign—"

"Oh," Miss Somers said. "That. I had to go out to deliver a cat. Nothing would do but I take it that very afternoon. You know how people are."

"Well—" Pam said.

"And I've nobody to leave," Miss Somers said. "The young man I had got another offer and—for the little time I'll keep the shop going—"

"Not *Winkle!*" Pam said and to this Madeline Somers quite simply, if understandably, said "Huh?" Pam explained—explained that, for some reason, she thought of the little Siamese queen as "Winkle."

"I don't know why," Pam said, to avoid going again into that.

"Heavens no," Miss Somers said. "An all-white Manx. A much more expensive cat. Otherwise— You and Mr. North have decided you want her?"

"I'm not really sure," Pam said. "But—probably. Anyway, I'd like to look at her again and—" Pam almost said, "Talk to her," which was more or less what she meant. It is important to talk to cats, and especially to Siamese cats. But Madeline Somers, in spite of her trade, might be one of those who do not know this. "Examine her a little more carefully," Pam said, keeping it simple, as she always tries to do.

"Of course," Madeline Somers said. "You want to be sure. You'll both come around, then?"

Only she, Pam explained, and did not go into the matter of Mr. Simpson. They had talked it over, and her husband was perfectly willing for her to decide for both of them. "Although," Pam said, "we're both very fond of them." Miss Somers might—although for some reason Pam a little doubted it—want to be sure that her cats found congenial homes.

"I would like to know today," Miss Somers said. "If it's at all possible. There's someone else who's quite interested, I think."

"This morning," Pam promised.

There were, then, certain small delays—Dorian Weigand telephoned, to suggest a dropping by for cocktails, and they found several other things to talk about; Pam remembered she had forgotten to make an appointment at Antoine's and this, which should have been quickly accomplished, took rather a long time, owing to switchboard difficulties. (Pam was connected with the fur department and after that with junior misses. Saks' switchboard was having a bad day.) So it was ten thirty and a few minutes more when Pam closed the apartment door behind her and walked the few steps down the corridor which took her to the elevator. She was waiting for the elevator to rise to the occasion when she heard the telephone ringing in her apartment.

Pam cannot ignore telephones. One never knows. She hurried back the few steps and fished in her bag for her key container, while

[163]

beyond the door the bell harshly, repetitiously, summoned. Pam fished with growing anxiety. It would be at the bottom; it would be under everything. It would— She found it. She opened the door. And the telephone rang its last.

Pam knew it had; she had been almost certain that it would, being familiar with the habits of telephones. She took the receiver up and listened. It buzzed at her—buzzed its triumph. "Fooled you again," the buzz said. Pam put the receiver back in its cradle—put it back jarringly. Serve it right to be jarred.

Ten thirty-seven it was then, as Pam stepped into the elevator and pushed the proper button. She hoped Miss Somers would really put a "hold" on Winkle.

***

At eleven thirty, Captain William Weigand shuffled papers, initialing where required, taking from "In" basket and depositing in "Out" basket. Some of the papers had to do with the Blanchard case; most did not. There is seldom one murder at a time on the west side of Manhattan—since Blanchard had died, a young woman had been knifed to death (probably by her estranged husband), Big Nose Brancenti (so distinguished from his cousin, Little Nose Brancenti) had been filled with bullets at the wheel of his parked Cadillac. The gangsters were coming back.

"Here we are," Mullins said, coming into the office, and holding papers out. He gave the papers—three sheets, two and a half of them used by the typist; the first two initialed "G.L." at the bottom, the last signed "Graham Latham"—signed very legibly, very neatly.

Bill read Latham's formal statement. It did not vary from Latham's oral answers; boiled them down, kept them in sequence. Concise and clear—that was Graham Latham. There was no confession of murder. Bill had not really expected one—one either false or true, in either case to exonerate a girl. So, Latham was not that scared— if for a few seconds that scared, had simmered down. Bill nodded,

[164]

and Mullins left. Almost at once he returned with Latham, who walked stiffly; who, when directed, sat carefully; whose eyes were shrewd, speculative, in a tanned face.

"Very clear," Bill said. "They told you it might, if needed, be used in evidence?"

Latham merely nodded.

"You read it over," Bill said. "Found nothing you wanted to change in any way?"

"Nothing," Latham said. "Nothing I can think of." He paused. "Now," he said.

Which was, Bill Weigand thought, a way of saying that circumstances might alter purposes. But all he said was, "Right, Mr. Latham."

"So?"

"We won't take any more of your time," Bill said. Then he paused; smiled faintly. "Now," he said. "You won't get lost, I'm sure."

"Couldn't if I wanted to, eh?"

Bill shrugged slightly.

"And," he said, "you'll let us know what you hear from your daughter?"

"Well—"

"I'm getting in touch with the Los Angeles police," Weigand said, his tone noncommittal.

"Listen—"

"No," Bill said. "Not suggesting any action. Now. You'll let us know what you hear?"

"Probably," Latham said, and stood up slowly, painfully.

"Long hot baths help sometimes," Bill said, and stood up too.

"I've heard," Latham said, with scepticism—scepticism which, on the basis of Bill Weigand's own experience, was fully justified. Latham went, slowly, carefully, a man trying to glide.

"You thought he might sing?" Mullins said. "To protect the girl?"

Bill shook his head.

"Not yet, anyway," he said. "And—I rather doubt he'll need to, Mullins. And whose canary have you been eating?"

"O.K.," Mullins said. "Could be this man says he's a doctor. Cat doctor?"

"Gebhardt," Weigand said. "You mean—he isn't?"

"Oh," Mullins said, "sure he is. Got a place on Park Avenue, like he says. Must be money in sick cats."

Bill waited. Mullins held out to him a memo form—a memo from the Traffic Department.

A summons for illegal parking had been placed under the windshield wiper of a pale yellow Cadillac, standing within inches of a fire hydrant. License checked out as belonging to Dr. Oscar Gebhardt, residing in Chappaqua, with offices at—Park Avenue.

Place of violation—the block between Fifth Avenue and University Place on East Tenth Street. Time of violation—4:10 P.M. the previous day.

"Five minutes' walk from where Ackerman got it," Mullins said. "Three, if he hurried." He looked at Bill Weigand with hope in his blue eyes. "Man could walk pretty fast to grab on to two hundred grand," Mullins suggested, holding out another silver platter.

The platter, Bill thought, was by no means empty. Its contents were, actually, more substantial than a hunch—a hunch resting, admittedly, on a foundation of thin air.

"Right," Bill said. "Ask him about it, sergeant. Ask him if he hurried. Or, send Nate, if you like."

"The pleasure," Sergeant Mullins said, as he stood up, "the pleasure will be mine, loot."

The telephone rang and Bill picked it up, at the same time motioning Mullins to be on his way. "L.A.'s on," Bill was told and said, "Right," and then, "Morning, captain. Didn't take you long."

"Happened it came to me," a police captain three thousand miles away told Bill. "Happened I'd handled it. About this girl—"

XVI

PAM WENT DOWN the two steps from sidewalk level and tinkled her way into *the breeders' nook*. The first room—the display room—was empty, as it had been before. "With you in a minute," Madeline Somers called, evidently from the next room, and there was the scratchy sound of paper being torn. Pam, from long experience, immediately identified Miss Somers's activity. Miss Somers was changing cats' toilet pans, shredding fresh newspaper to replace the old. "It's Mrs. North," Pam called back. "No hurry." She sat. She heard more paper torn. A cat shop, she thought, must run to a good deal of newspaper.

There was then the sound of something being opened—of course, a cage. There was the sound of something being closed. Miss Somers came through the curtains, wearing the same beige-colored suit, clutching a small Siamese, who spoke, as before. Miss Somers said, "Good morning. Isn't it a lovely day? Here's the little doll."

She started to put the little doll on the display pedestal.

"Let me have her," Pam said.

"Well," Miss Somers said, and hesitated. "She's shedding, you know." She looked at Pam's fall suit—a darkish suit, not colored to match Siamese. Pam held out her hands. She said, "Aren't they always?" and accepted the little cat, who turned and looked up at her. Not really pointed. And beautifully colored eyes. "Nice baby," Pam said. "Pretty baby." She put the cat on her lap, and began to run knowing fingers over the small, but wiry and muscular, little body. No flabbiness—sometimes even young cats—

The young cat—possibly the future Winkle—began to purr, mis-

[167]

taking palpation for caress. "Pretty baby," Pam said, and scratched the cat behind the right ear. Miss Somers looked on.

"Wasn't it," Pam said, "dreadful about poor Mr. Ackerman?"

She said it to say something—said it because she felt that Miss Somers was expecting her to say something, and she was not yet quite ready to say yes, they would take the little cat. Also, of course, Ackerman had been an acquaintance—an associate, really—of Miss Somers. It seemed only proper to note his passing.

"Ackerman?" Miss Somers said. She said the name as if she had never heard it before.

"*Floyd* Ackerman," Pam said, as one who chooses among many. Blankness remained on Miss Somers's pink, firm face. Then it faded. "Oh," she said. "The antivivisection man. What about him?"

"Dead," Pam said. "It seems he hanged himself. Unless somebody did it for him."

"Goodness," Miss Somers said. "The poor man."

Her tone was one of entire detachment. A customer wished to discuss a topic of no interest; a proper saleswoman feigned interest. And Pam North felt herself blinking, inwardly. She continued to probe the cat's supple body, to the cat's audible pleasure.

"I thought you knew him," Pam said. "That's the reason I mentioned it. Wasn't that he here yesterday?"

"Yesterday?" Miss Somers repeated. "Floyd Ackerman?"

"I thought—" Pam said. "I was wrong, obviously. A thin man? With very large glasses?"

Miss Somers shook her head, as if Pam were speaking of the incomprehensible, and in a foreign language.

"I don't remember any—" she said, and interrupted herself. "Oh," she said. "I do remember. That was a man to fix the refrigerator. I have to keep perishable food, of course. For them." She gestured toward the curtains. "The thing broke down. What ever made you think it was this Mr. Ackerman?"

[168]

Pam searched her mind. What, in effect, had? A connection—

"Oh," she said. "He'd taken a manuscript to my husband once. And his name came up—because Mr. Blanchard had written a letter about him in the *Times*—and Jerry—Jerry's my husband—described him."

Miss Somers shook her head. The shake indicated that this seemed remote, inadequate.

"Oh yes," Pam said. "Dr. Gebhardt—you know Gebby?"

Miss Somers smiled, this time. The smile was that of a woman who, after treading fog, has got solid earth under her feet.

"I certainly do," she said. "Wonderful vet, Gebby. And such a delightful—" Again she broke off. "Only," she said, "what about him?"

"He," Pam said, "said you were a member of this committee. Mr. Ackerman's committee. I suppose I just put two and two—" She shrugged slim shoulders, more or less in apology.

"The Committee Against Cruelty," Miss Somers said. "I am, as a matter of fact. I got several letters asking me to join and finally—well, it was only five dollars." She paused again. "Actually," she said, as one who confesses, "I thought it might be good for business. People who are interested in cats—some of them might—well, you see how it is."

The little cat seemed to have gone to sleep on Pam's lap. Pam stroked the top of the cat's head, gently.

"Of course," Pam said. "About the baby here—"

"I never laid eyes on this Mr. Ackerman," Miss Somers said. "What did you mean somebody did it *for* him? There wasn't any—you mean somebody *killed* him?"

There was the to-be-expected shocked disbelief on the word "killed."

"Probably," Pam said, "I shouldn't have said that. There wasn't anything—" For an instant the words echoed in her mind. She had been about to say that there had been nothing about that possibility in the newspaper accounts. Had Miss Somers been about to say the same thing? Nonsense. Miss Somers had, clearly, not heard of Ackerman's taking off until Pam mentioned it. So—

"I really shouldn't have," Pam said. "The police obviously don't—"

"Oh," Miss Somers said. "I'd almost forgotten that you and Mr. North sometimes work with—you mean they think it was murder? Not suicide? This friend of yours—this detective—"

There was a change in Miss Somers's attitude. She was interested now, Pam thought. Of course, people are interested in murder stories. And, probably even more, in feeling themselves on the inside of things, possessors of knowledge hidden from the general.

"It's only a possibility," Pam said. "Probably by now they don't even think that any longer. They have to consider all possibilities, of course. Even the most unlikely. About the baby—"

"Oh yes. Forgotten what you came about, almost, hadn't we? She is a doll, isn't she. Muscular little thing, isn't she?" Miss Somers had not, clearly, mistaken palpation for caressing. "I'm sure you and your husband will be delighted with her. Pity he couldn't come with you. I always think it's best if both—well, parents—" Her tone apologized for the possible sentimentality of the word—"agree about a kitten. He knew you were coming, of course?"

The question ticked in Pam's mind. Did this sturdy, pink-faced woman think she was sneaking off behind Jerry's back and— Nonsense, Pam told herself. An entirely reasonable enquiry, deserving an entirely reasonable answer.

"Only that I might," she said. "You see, we didn't know whether you'd be open. If you weren't, I might have got the car and gone to a cattery. There's one up near Chappaqua Gebby says is very reliable."

"I know the one you mean," Miss Somers said. "I've bought several there myself. They do run a little more to Burmese, of course. I'm glad—*watch her!*"

[170]

The warning came a cat's leap too late. Pam had removed her hands from the little Siamese queen. The cat, who had seemed to be asleep, had, evidently, been waiting—waiting to use the smooth strong muscles, to take the exercise a young cat needs. She was out of reach in an instant; she was out of the room in two. She darted between the curtains, tail high, a cat on her own again.

"*Goodness!*" Pam North said, and darted after her. "Can she get out—I mean—"

For a moment, Madeline Somers did not follow. She turned, she watched Pam—watched until Pam had disappeared between the curtains.

"There's a back door," she called, then. "I think it's closed but—I'll get that. You—look under things."

Pam was already looking under things—in the middle room she was looking under cages. Cages lined either side of the room—a dozen cages in all. Only three had cats in them, Pam noticed, as she crawled under—as she said, "Here baby. Pretty baby," and then, as a tryout, "Come here, Winkle. Come *here.*"

The little cat did not. Pam crawled out and stood for a moment, looking at three cats in cages, before crawling under the cages against the other wall. A long-hair with an amazing tail—probably a Coon cat. The male Siamese she had been shown the day before. And—an all-white Manx. Apparently Miss Somers had held two of a kind—two of an uncommon kind, at that. But the issue now was the cat who might, in time, become Winkle. Pam went under the other row of cages.

No cat. A pile of newspapers, ready for future shredding. The uppermost with a three-column cut of wrestling lion cubs. A familiar picture—of course, on the split page of that morning's *Times.* It was odd that Miss Somers—

"She's out here," Madeline Somers called. She called from the room beyond. "Come and help."

[171]

Pam went. She went quickly; went through a doorway into a much larger room. "Close the door quick," Madeline Somers said, and Pam closed the door, quick, behind her.

The room she closed herself and Madeline Somers—and, it was to be assumed, a small, quick Siamese—into was, clearly, the combination office and shipping room of *the breeders' nook*. In the rear, under a window, near a door (which, Pam supposed, led to a back yard) there was a desk, with a filing cabinet beside it. Along either side, for almost the full length of the room, there were wide counters. The one on the left—under which Madeline Somers was looking, with a flashlight to aid her—held equipment for those concerned with cats. There were cat beds (which it was unlikely, Pam thought, any cat would ever use) and carriers for cats. There were boxes containing proprietary substitutes for torn up newspaper; there were half a dozen disassembled scratching posts, squared posts and wide bases waiting to be wedged together. There were wooden shipping cages, for cats destined to travel by express. There was a small carton of catnip mice; a larger carton which, from the stenciled marking, contained "Kitty Houses." Whatever, Pam thought briefly, they might be.

The counter along the opposite wall was less laden—a counter, Pam thought, again briefly—set aside for the actual wrapping of outgoing cat accessories. Pam began to look under it for the little cat.

The space under this counter was almost entirely occupied by cardboard cartons of various sizes—emptied cartons which had, evidently, once contained cat toys; larger cartons, stenciled with manufacturers' names, in which scratching posts had arrived; two cartons as large as wardrobe trunks, in which bulky merchandise—cat carriers, at a guess, or cat cages—had been sent to *the breeders' nook*.

"Here baby," Pam began to say, and began to crawl in among the cartons. "Nice baby."

Here the little cat would be, if anywhere. Boxes—all kinds of boxes; empty boxes, most of them with hinged tops open. Into and out of boxes an agile cat—and this one was all of that—could go indefinitely, the searcher always a box or two behind. Pam began to haul boxes from under the counter, shake them, set them aside and upside down. No cat.

"The little devil!" Madeline Somers said, from behind Pam, apparently from under something. Pam hauled out cartons, piling them behind her. It was dark under there. What she needed was a flashlight. She came out.

Miss Somers had also come out. She was standing with her back to the counter, looking at Pam.

"Probably in one of these," Pam said, indicating, and, at the same time, beginning to look about for a flashlight. She looked first on the counter under which she had searched—the almost bare counter. Above the counter, set in brackets, was a wide roll of heavy wrapping paper; next it, on a spindle also set in brackets, a cylinder of heavy—very heavy, ropelike—binding cord. Brown cord, a quarter of an inch or more in diameter—

The free end of the cord—the thin rope—had a loop knotted in it. The knot had a name—the name swirled, beyond reach, in Pam North's swirling mind. Just now—almost just now—

Pam whirled from the counter.

"A *bowline!*" she said, and was conscious that she spoke loudly. "That's what they call it—a *bowline. That's what*—"

She stopped. Madeline Somers was holding the square club of a scratching post in her hands—lifting it in her hands. Pam could see the hardened muscles in Madeline Somers's sturdy forearms and whirled and ran toward the door she had come through.

"*You little snoop!*" Madeline Somers said, loudly. "You prying little—"

Pam reached the door and tugged at the knob, and knew that she hadn't time for that. She started to turn to face the woman with the square club. But only started—

***

He had cast into thin air—more precisely, perhaps, into smog— and caught something. Which was gratifying. Bill Weigand looked at his penciled notes. The question remained—what had he caught? He tapped the desk top with fingers, tapping out a rhythm. A rhythm of enquiry, of speculation.

His last question on the telephone had been whether the man he talked to was sure. He had got a patient sigh; it had been suggested to him that he, a cop, ought to know better than that. He had been told, once more, that there was nothing to suggest that the girl had not caught her heel in a loose metal edging of a stair tread and pitched, headlong, down a steep flight of stairs and broken her neck at the foot of them.

"We checked it out," the captain in Los Angeles said, again. "And the insurance investigator checked it out—checked it out hard and long. Nobody wanted to sue, as it turned out, but they weren't taking chances. Somebody turns up and—wow! Because the tread *was* loose, and the owners *had* been notified and hadn't got around to it. If the Rush girl had had hungry relatives— Anyway, no soap—high heels and a loose metal strip. They couldn't get away from it. Only, they did get away with funeral expenses, because no relatives turned up. So—?"

Bill had thanked him and now tapped his fingers on his desk. He had had, admitted to himself he had had, higher hopes. Madeline Somers was in it—there was that. But, apparently, she *wasn't* in it, not *really* in it, and there was that, too. Bill Weigand reviewed.

Two women sharing an apartment in Los Angeles—a walk-up, they on the second floor. Had shared it for a week, only, and that— Bill Weigand used his fingers now to count back—and that almost a

[174]

year and a half ago. May of the previous year. A woman named Louise Rush; a woman named Madeline Somers. Neither employed; both recently come to Los Angeles. Both looking, but apparently in an unhurried fashion, for employment. No immediate financial pressure on them, evidently. The apartment had been reasonably expensive. They had, for all anybody could discover, done themselves rather well.

They had started out on a May evening to go to dinner, Louise had gone first. She had caught her heel on the metal strip, and plunged down. Madeline had clutched for her, missed; had hurried down after her and found her friend dead; had called—had screamed —for help.

There had never, really, been any suspicion against Madeline Somers. She profited nothing. The girls had, from what little could be learned of them—they had not had time, apparently, to make friends who could be asked—been on the best of terms. At the restaurant they had eaten in most frequently, a waitress had got to know them by sight. She said they seemed to get on swell. If anything, the last couple of times before it happened, they had seemed unusually gay. Laughing and joking and lighted up. She had thought that one, or both of them, had got good jobs or something.

The wall between their apartment and the next had not been thick—not too thick to baffle sound. While they were dressing to go out on the last evening of Louise Rush's life—the woman in the next-door apartment assumed they were dressing—they had been talking lickety-split, and laughing like anything.

The insurance investigators had worked hard on this; worked hard to find some way in which Madeline Somers gained by the other's death. They had come up with a wall a good deal thicker, more impervious, than that through which the two youngish women had been heard laughing.

The loose strip had been reported—reported two days before the accident; reported by Madeline Somers, who had said that the management had better do something before somebody fell down the stairs and broke his neck. Used those words, prophetically. The words anybody might use, making need of a repair seem urgent. Nothing to go on there. The management had checked, found conditions as described. A man was to have come the next morning to replace the faulty stripping. (And had. Which did Louise Rush no good.)

Madeline had told her simple story, and told it straightforwardly. So far as the captain Weigand had talked to—he had been a lieutenant then—could tell, and he had interviewed Madeline Somers, who seemed greatly shocked by what had happened. She and Louise had known each other only briefly, but Louise had been a lovely person. It was a terrible thing to have happened.

"Convinced me," the Los Angeles captain said. "Convinced the insurance guys, who wanted something different."

Miss Somers had stayed on at the apartment for only a few days. Then she had moved away—first, briefly, to a residence hotel; afterward to New York. When she was established in New York, she had sent back a forwarding address. There had, however, been little mail to forward. "Sort of a loney," the Los Angeles captain had guessed.

Bill Weigand considered. That part of it came together— Alex Somers, "Cousin Alex," had died about two years before. Six months would have been quite long enough for John Blanchard, as administrator, to discover that Madeline Somers was the heir—or one of the heirs—to notify her, to— The two women had seemed especially gay during the couple of days just before Louise Rush died. Because Madeline Somers had learned she was to inherit money? And offered to let Louise help spend some of it when it arrived? Enough, certainly, to make them cheerful—notably cheerful.

It worked out well enough. Miss Somers, her friend dead, had come to New York to be—call it nearer the source of supply. Had opened her cat shop to pass the time of waiting. Conceivably, got an advance against the inheritance? That should not have been impossible. Or, had enough money of her own to open the shop? Quite possible, also.

It worked out well enough. The trouble was that it did not really work out *to* anything. A sad happening in Madeline Somers's past. No evident connection with the—

For the love of God, Bill Weigand thought. Call yourself a detective!

He reached for the telephone. He made three calls. The first was to the North apartment. He was answered, this time—answered by Martha. Mrs. North was not at home. She had left a note—she always left notes when she left before Martha arrived. (Otherwise Martha might be worried or, at any rate, puzzled.) This note read: "Gone to look at a new cat." Martha read it to Bill Weigand, and was thanked. She said, "Mrs. North's all right, captain?" and Bill said, "Sure," and hung up to call again. This time he called the office of North Books, Inc. Mr. North had taken an author out to lunch. Where he had not said; when he would be back he had not said. It could be pretty late, Miss Abigail Clark told Weigand, speaking from experience. Sometimes these lunches with authors— The third call was to precinct, asking cooperation.

XVII

Captain William Weigand parked his Buick—which looked like any Buick of its year and model, if one did not notice the rather long radio antenna—at a meter space on Madison Avenue. Law-abiding, he put a coin in the meter and turned the knob. He walked, a man in no evident hurry, half a block and a man in slacks and odd jacket, walking toward him, also in no apparent hurry, said, "Happen to have a match on you?" Bill gave him matches. "O.K.," the man said, "only looks like nobody's home." He sauntered on. After half a dozen strides he apparently decided he was going in the wrong direction, and turned, and sauntered back.

Bill went down two steps from the sidewalk level and looked at a door—at a lowered shade with one word on it. The word was "Closed." The man in slacks and jacket stopped at the top of the two steps and Bill turned. "Thanks for the matches," the man said, and held out the folder, which Bill took. "Covered in the rear," the man said. "Station wagon backed up to the loading dock." Bill said, "Right. Thanks," and the man walked on, in no hurry—and not far.

Bill reached a finger toward a bell-push beside the door, and stayed the finger. Pamela North had gone to look at a new cat. A harmless enough activity, surely. But—Pamela North, engaged in reasonably harmless activities, now and then gets herself into spots of trouble. So far, she had got herself out of them. But still—

There is a small instrument, recently perfected, which greatly simplifies an ancient procedure. It is, authority hopes, limited to the uses of policemen and locksmiths. It is by no means in general issue even to policemen. Weigand had never used his before, except

[178]

to try it out after a demonstration. This was, he decided, a good—if highly illegal—time to begin.

It was not, of course, as quick as a key would have been. Nobody had contended that it would be. But it was really hardly any trouble at all to use. Having used it, Bill opened the door quietly, and quietly moved inside.

He moved into an empty room—a room like a living room, but with a pedestal in the center of the room. Nothing on the pedestal. Bill stood still and listened, and heard nothing. Bill parted curtains and went into another room; this one with cages on either side—and a few cats in cages. The cats looked at him. A Siamese cat spoke in welcome, and Bill froze.

Nothing happened. It began to appear that there was, indeed, nobody home—that the bird had flown. (If the bird sought, which was still by no means certain.) On the other hand, Siamese cats talk a good deal, some of them to themselves. People who know them get used to this, may pay no attention. Bill stood and listened. He heard nothing and moved on across the room—moved with what he trusted was an appropriately catlike tread. He reached a door and stood close to it.

He heard something then—heard from beyond the door a shuffling sound and then, faintly, a human "uh!", soft, as if a reaction to physical effort. Bill turned the knob of the door, loosened the catch as silently as he could, and pulled the door open as quickly as he could.

A sturdy woman in a beige-colored silk suit had, for an instant, her back to him—for that instant she was still shoving at a very large, evidently quite heavy, cardboard carton. A carton as big as a wardrobe trunk. A carton lashed around with heavy brown cord. She was pushing it toward the rear of a long room.

The tableau ended in the instant Bill saw it—ended with the sound of the opening door. The sturdy woman whirled. Her face was pink—pink, Bill supposed, from the effort of her shoving.

"How did you—" the woman said, loudly. "We're cl—" She did not finish. Mind had caught up with speech.

She moved away from the big carton. She was not touching it. And the carton, untouched, swayed uncertainly, bumpily, from side to side.

For an instant she looked at the moving carton. Not at Bill Weigand.

"Police," Bill said, and started toward her, and she ran—ran heavily, ran down the long room toward a door at the end of it.

"Miss Rush!" Bill said, and did not raise his voice. "It's no good. You'd better—"

She did not stop. She ran on; she tugged open a door at the end of the room.

And then she stopped.

"Going some place?" the broad-shouldered man she faced said. "Don't want her to, do we, captain?"

Bill said, "No," and said it over his shoulder. He was looking for a knife. He found it on a counter, under a spindle of heavy brown cord—three-eighths of an inch in diameter, three ply.

"Doesn't want you to go any place," the broad-shouldered man said to the sturdy woman, from whose face pinkness now had faded. He moved toward her. She backed into the room.

Bill slashed at the brown cord around the big carton. Holes had been cut in the top of the carton—air holes. The last lashing fell away and Bill tore at the top flaps of the carton, which opened to his tugging.

Pamela North, doubled into a kind of knot, glared up at him. He had never seen such angry eyes, Bill thought, and reached for her.

A stocking ran through her mouth, was knotted behind her head. Bill, careful now, cut that first.

"Awful woman," Pam North said. "Going to take me to an accident. It hurts."

What hurt—what would have hurt anyone—was the bite of cord —the brown, the ropelike, cord—with which she was bound; with which she was bound into a knot; a shape to fit the capacity of the carton. Bill's knife slashed.

"I tried to make it bump," Pam North said, sitting on the floor, rubbing her ankles. (The bonds had started there, been drawn tightest there—had started with the line passed through the fixed loop of a bowline to make a running loop.) "Did it bump?"

"Yes, Pam," Bill Weigand said. "It bumped."

"She—?" Pam said.

"Behind you."

Pam whirled, as if on a turntable.

"All I came for was to look at a cat," Pam North said. "That was all—Miss Somers."

Pam is customarily soft of voice. She made the woman's name an epithet.

"No, Pam," Bill said above her. "Not Miss Somers. Dead a long time, Miss Somers is. Fell downstairs and broke her neck, didn't she, Miss Rush? Miss Louise Rush."

The sturdy woman, whose arms were now gripped firmly from behind, did not say anything at all.

Pam twisted to look up at Bill Weigand.

"Rush?" she said. Bill nodded his head. "Rush?" Pam said again, disbelief—incomprehension—still in her voice.

"Uh-huh," Bill said. "That's the name they'll try her under."

***

"Are you sure you're all right?" Jerry asked, with anxiety which had diminished only a little. "Yes, dear," Pam said, for what she thought must be the twentieth time. "I keep telling you—"

[181]

Jerry crossed the room and knelt by her chair so that he could put his arms around her.

"Perfectly all right," Pam said, when her lips were again available. "The post had carpet on it, you know."

Jerry tilted back and sat on his heels.

"Some day," he said, and spoke darkly. "Some day, you're going to get yourself killed."

She said, "*Jerry!*" to that. She said, "All I went to do was to look at a cat. We agreed on that. Didn't we?"

"Well—"

"And it's not my fault if she—this Miss Rush, only I still keep thinking Somers—if she thought I was—" Pam paused. "Detecting," she said. "Actually, I was as innocent as—as Winkle." She paused, obviously in thought. "I think no about her," Pam said. "She's a doll and everything, but I'd always think of cartons." She paused again. "The insides of cartons," she said, amplifying. "I'd never thought about them before. Dark. And very stuffy, after the first few minutes."

She had been, at a guess, in the carton for at least half an hour —perhaps longer. In it while it was tilted back and forth as the sturdy woman they would have to begin to think of as Louise Rush had tied heavy brown cord around it; in it, then, for some time longer, while nothing happened. "While she went to get the station wagon," Pam said, going over it again. "To take me to an accident."

She had only been knocked out for a few seconds—actually not "out," in the precise sense, for any time at all. "It was always sort of blurry," Pam said. That was after the sturdy woman had hit her, from behind, with the square club of the scratching post—the padded club. When the blur ended, she was already partly tied up, and gagged with the stocking.

[182]

"My *own* stocking!" Pam said, with remembered, with renewed, indignation.

"Yes, Pam," Jerry said, and stood up. "Very dirty billiards, to use your own stocking." He went back to his own chair, his own martini. Pam sipped hers.

"All the time she talked," Pam said. "Called me all sorts of names —snoop and I don't know what all. And all I'd gone for was to look at the cat. If she hadn't been so wrong—thinking I was a detective when I wasn't—she might—would she have got away with it?"

Jerry didn't know. He assumed not, since Bill had already, obviously, been on to it. Probably, the misconception in Miss Somers's —no, Miss Rush's—mind only hurried things along. Bill would tell them more when he arrived. Which ought to be any—

She had not only called Pam names. She had, although not in precise terms—"just you wait and see, you little snoop"—described Pam's future, which was to have been brief. She had said this as she tilted the big carton on its side and rolled Pam into it, and set it upright again.

Pam was to be taken off to have an accident. She could not, obviously, have it there, in the shop. And she could not die until she had it. "They've got ways of telling," the sturdy woman had told Pam, needlessly. Pam was not sure that Louise Rush had worked out her own plans in any detail; suspected she was making them up as she went along. At any rate, when she was putting down the top flaps of the carton—after saying, "All tucked in, dearie?" in a very unpleasant voice—she had said, "Got it! Let him and that girl of his explain it."

"I thought—" Pam said, and paused. "Actually," she said, "I don't know I did, then. I was too scared. Don't think I wasn't scared."

"I don't," Jerry said. "Latham and his daughter? Have your accident near where they live?"

"I think so," Pam said. "Maybe she's talked. Told Bill. Maybe—"

[183]

The doorbell rang. It would be Bill Weigand; it was Bill Weigand. He still looked tired, but now in a different way—now he looked tired but satisfied. He would very much like a drink; seated with it, he proved his statement. It was after he had taken a longish swallow and put the glass down on the table beside him that Jerry said, "Well? Has she?"

Bill shook his head. Except to deny that she was Louise Rush, the sturdy woman had not said anything at all. She seemed, Bill told them, a little dazed. She had been booked as Louise Rush, alias Madeline Somers, and booked on a charge of felonious assault. "To start with," Bill said, and nodded at Pam and smiled and said that she had been most helpful. "Astute of you to get knocked about," he said, gravely. "Gave us a handle—a handle to hold her with."

Pam said, "*You!*" She said, "I just went to look at a cat." She said, finally, that she supposed the next thing he would say was that she had used her head. She rubbed the head she had used. She said, "Big as a goose egg."

"All the same," Bill Weigand said, "the point was what she thought, was afraid of. Not what was true. Thought you were closing in on her, was stampeded by her own fear; by her own knowledge of what she had to fear."

"Of course," Pam said, "to give myself credit—at the very end, she was right. Or partly right. I did think the cord answered the description. I did say, in effect, 'Lookee! A bowline as I live and breathe!' So— She killed them both?"

"Right," Bill said. "And, probably, a woman into the bargain—eighteen months or so ago, in Los Angeles. By pushing her down a flight of stairs. A woman named Madeline Somers. A woman whose place she had decided to take."

He told them of that. He said that the Los Angeles police, and the insurance detectives also, would now have another and longer

[184]

look at the circumstances surrounding the death of a youngish woman incorrectly identified as Louise Rush—*by* Louise Rush.

They, and the New York police, would dig back, now—now that they knew what they were digging for. Bill had no doubt that the process would take time; no doubt that it would be successful. "Nobody really covers a past," he said. "Everybody leaves traces. No impersonation is worth a damn once it is suspected." Also, he thought it highly likely that the woman in jail would crack. Because she was the type that panicked. She emotionally denied what she had no need to deny; she might, therefore, be expected emotionally to admit what she was not forced to admit. The two courses of action were of the same nature.

"Like," Pam said, "denying she knew Ackerman. That he had been there."

"Right," Bill said. "Knowing Ackerman didn't convict her of anything. It was foolish to deny it—got her nowhere. And we won't, I imagine, have much difficulty in proving she did know him. For what it's worth. Another thing—you look at her, Pam, and say, in effect, 'Look! A bowline!' and all she has to do is say, 'So what? Thousands of people use bowlines.' Which is perfectly true. But instead—panic."

"Conscience doth," Pam said. "She found out that Madeline Somers was going to have money coming, decided to impersonate her and get the money? Killing her first, of course. Did she arrange to get friendly with Miss Somers because she knew Miss Somers had money coming? Or find it out afterward?"

"I haven't the faintest idea," Bill told them both, and finished his drink and looked at it. Jerry North said, "O.K., loot," and Pam said, "By the way, where is he?"

"Getting the digging under way," Bill said. "Since he discovered your Gebhardt was helping a cat have kittens. In an apartment on Tenth Street." He explained that briefly.

"Poor Mullins," Pam said.

She returned to the main issue. She supposed that John Blanchard had found out about the impersonation and got killed for his knowledge. How? That Ackerman had found out about the first murder and got killed for that knowledge. How had he found out?

"Ackerman saw someone getting out of the elevator Sunday morning," Bill said. "The woman, we can be pretty sure, he knew as Madeline Somers. He tried, probably, to put the bite on. Got to thinking it over, lost his nerve and called you, Jerry. Not in time, as it turned out. Probably, she—"

"There are," Pam said, "a good many probablys, aren't there?"

Bill smiled, he nodded his head. He said there always were; that everything started, always, with "probably." Except, of course, things seen—like assault on the person of one Pamela North.

As to how Blanchard found out—

Bill told of two letters among Blanchard's papers: Of a letter signed by Madeline Somers, authorizing expenditure for a tombstone; of a letter signed (or swirled) by Paul Flagler, handwriting expert, saying, in effect, that Blanchard had something there. Bill waited. Jerry considered; shook his head. Pam's eyes dimmed with thought. Then she said, "Oh, of course. But where were the other letters?"

The other letters—the letters which must have been written by the real Madeline Somers, letters which presumably established her identity—those had, probably—"all right, beyond doubt"—been taken and destroyed by Louise Rush. After Blanchard, who had got Flagler's letter Saturday and at once summoned "Madeline Somers" to explain why the signature on her latest letter did not match other signatures, had showed them to her. After she had crushed Blanchard's skull with the base of a scratching post.

"Why not the tombstone letter?" Jerry said. "For that matter, the letter from Flagler?"

The "tombstone" letter, by itself, did her no harm. Actually, its existence was, with Blanchard out of the way, the final distribution of the Somers estate inevitably in other hands, of advantage to Louise Rush. It proved that Madeline Somers had been accepted as an heir. As to the Flagler letter—

Blanchard had filed it under "F," Bill told them. She apparently didn't look under "F." There would have been no reason for Blanchard to name Flagler. 'A handwriting expert' was all he needed to say. He didn't have to prove what he said. What he said went, as far as she was concerned. When he needed Flagler would have been when he brought charges of attempted fraud.

It was with Flagler, incidentally, that Mullins was getting the digging under way. Flagler had, obviously, returned the questioned documents. Now— Bill interrupted himself. He said that there had been a point on which he had been decidedly slow on the uptake. The "tombstone" letter had been folded once for an envelope of one size, folded again for one of another. Therefore—obviously mailed twice. He had missed that, at first—

To get back. Flagler would not have the letters with the signatures which failed to match. But he would remember them, would be able to describe them. Once they were absolutely sure of that, could document that, they would try it on Louise Rush, alias Madeline Somers. It might be the wedge. If not—if not, something else would be. Something in the past, since nobody covers the—

"Bill!" Pam said. "There wouldn't have been *two* all-white Manxes. Nobody would stock two when they're not that popular and must be very expensive and—"

She was asked to wait a minute. She waited, politely. She was urged to continue, filling in as she went. She said, "Oh." She said that Miss Rush-Somers, in explaining where she had been the previous afternoon, had said that she was out delivering an all-white

Manx cat. "Instead of hanging poor Mr. Ackerman." But—there was an all-white Manx still in residence at *the breeders' nook*.

"Well—" Bill said, in doubt.

"Cats like that aren't anonymous," Pam said, firmly. "Rare. Registered. And—people keep records. She must have done herself, because the shop wasn't just what—what people call a cover. So—her own records. Two Manxes or only one? And catteries which breed Manxes and the cat associations and—oh, lots of things."

This time, Bill Weigand said, "Umm-m." Then he said, "Maybe." Then, after further thought, he said, "Right, Pam." He said that the duplication of white Manxes—

"With no tails at *all*."

With no tails at *all*, would be looked into. Meanwhile—

"The cats," Pam said. "Is somebody feeding them? All of them? The ones at the shop and Mr. Blanchard's and—"

She stopped, having run out of cats.

"Yes," Bill said. "We're feeding the ones in the shop. May have to enter them in evidence, you know. As for the Blanchard cats—Graham Latham's adopting them. Driving in this evening. Seems he does like cats and—"

"Hilda?" Pam said. "And the wounded tennis player?"

Marriage license applied for in Los Angeles County. Mears playing in the Pacific Coast tournament. Through the first round. Called twice on foot faults, but not on crucial points.

"I do hope," Pam North said, "that nothing drastic happens to *that* judge."